# NIGHT OF GLASS

# NIGHT OF GLASS

*by*

Philip Purser

**Dales Large Print Books**
Long Preston, North Yorkshire,
BD23 4ND, England.

British Library Cataloguing in Publication Data.

Purser, Philip
    Night of glass.

    A catalogue record of this book is
    available from the British Library

    ISBN    978-1-84262-811-9 pbk

First published in Great Britain in 1968
by Hodder & Stoughton Ltd.

Copyright © Philip Purser 1968

Cover illustration © Tanja Luther by arrangement with
Arcangel Images

Published in Large Print 2011 by arrangement with
Ostara Publishing

Dales Large Print is an imprint of Library Magna Books Ltd.

Printed and bound in Great Britain by
T.J. (International) Ltd., Cornwall, PL28 8RW

The Sailplane banked and turned with stiff, jerky deliberation, the umber fabric of its wings glowing as they tilted against the sun. When it steadied and began to rise on the warm up-draught the pilot gripped the control stick with his knees and once more raised the camera which hung from a sling round his neck. He worked hurriedly, aiming, pressing the release, winding on the film with long fingers, as the rectilinear pattern of buildings, roads and squares – even a narrow waterway ran ruler-straight – wheeled below. He saw the pink of upturned faces, the raw scars of fresh earthworks, a string of wagons on a rail siding. He dropped the camera back against his chest and concentrated on flying the sailplane. The long fingers which had twisted so impatiently at the film transport held the stick as lightly as a horseman's should hold the reins. Beneath a soft kid helmet, without goggles, the pilot's face was handsome, mask-like, strained. His eyes nervously scanned the sky above and behind him. He slipped the sling over his head, replaced the lens cap and carefully stowed the camera behind the little canvas seat. The air was cool on his cheek as he let the glider slide away to the south west.

# CHAPTER 1

Pickup ripped off the outer cellophane, opened the flap and let the twenty Players slide out still enclosed in their immaculate silver foil wrapping. He tipped the cigarettes into one hand and passed the foil to Stanley who, because he didn't smoke and didn't approve of smoking, wrinkled his doggy nose at the faintly clinging tobacco smell. Stanley worked the ball of his thumb over the folds until he had an unblemished – except for curling in the way that silver paper always curled when it was smoothed – oblong. With ruler and the rounded point of the scissors he marked it off into strips three-eighths of an inch wide and began to cut along the impressed lines. Pickup jostled the cigarettes back into the packet save for one which he put in his mouth. As he hunted in his pockets for a light he could feel further Stanley disapproval, for Stanley knew that he had just gone down to the cupboard under the stairs and helped himself to the packet from the half carton of packets which his mother had laid in, along with the tins of corned beef, sardines, Carnation milk, bottled apples and apricots, canister of tea, bag of flour, sack of potatoes, drum of Healthy Life biscuits, giant jar of Bovril and gross of Bryant and May's matches, against the prospect of air-raids.

Stanley said, 'You'll put them back?'

'I'll have to buy a new packet. They wouldn't keep, with the cellophane broken and no silver paper. They're supposed to be emergency rations. Hasn't your Mum gone in for that?' He said Mum and on purpose, because Stanley always referred to her as Mother.

Stanley laid the strip of gummed foil into a shallow depression he had gouged to one side of the model and dabbed it with his handkerchief. Pickup looked at it critically. It didn't look much like water, but of course you couldn't tell until it was all done. Making models was one of the enviable things about being an architectural student, and in his plodding way Stanley wasn't bad at it. He had done one of some proposed civic centre which had been included in an exhibition at the Williamson Art Gallery, admittedly not for the sake of the model itself but of the design (by one of Stanley's bosses) but it went to show ... certainly he knew all the dodges, like bits of dyed sponge for trees, and he actually had some carpentering skill, which Pickup notably lacked.

He said, 'The Czechs have mobilised, whatever that means exactly, which I'm never quite sure. It was on the wireless this morning. The French have ordered a partial mobilisation.' He heard the car turn in through the front gate, the slams – one, two – of the doors, and the boom of the front door as his parents came in from their Saturday afternoon shopping. Pickup lolled back and blew a plume of smoke towards the ceiling. He looked at the model aeroplanes on the mantelpiece, the last three he had made – or rather assembled from Frog kits – and the only three he still kept on display: the red de Havilland Comet that had won the Mildenhall–Melbourne air race in 1935, the Wellesley long-range aircraft with slender wings like outstretched arms, and tilting down menacingly from its pedestal, the German Stuka dive-bomber as crooked in outline as the Swastika emblazoned on its scarlet tail fin. He said in the Cambridge drawl which he put on at home when it suited him, 'And if old Chamberlain is going to keep flying to Germany I wish he'd go in a British plane instead of that Lockheed. What *will* the Germans think of a country which can't even make its own airliners?'

Stanley said predictably, 'If a person of that age goes in an aeroplane at all, to try and prevent war, I don't think we should criticise him for any reason.' When Pickup didn't reply he added ingratiatingly, 'What type should he have used in your opinion?'

Pickup said, 'Oh, I don't know. The Flamingo, perhaps; high-wing twin-engine. But it doesn't matter ... who cares?' He wanted to finish with this particular thought as quickly as he had introduced it. He was bored with it.

Stanley dabbed the last curling strip of foil into place. The silver inlay now ran the full length of the baseboard. He frowned at the too-smooth metallic effect and dipping his fingers in the half-dried residue which had collected round the rim of a little tin of enamel (matt earth, as used in the camouflage of military aircraft models) smeared brown shadows into the surface; suddenly it became a ditch or stream. He cut a little bridge from balsa strip, cemented the ends and dropped it into place across the stream in front of a little gatehouse. He said, 'What about this other moat, or whatever it is, that

14

runs round the whole thing?' He scratched at random in the tiny groove with the tip of the bradawl. 'To scale, it wouldn't be more than a sixteenth of an inch wide. It would be tiresome trying to do it with the silver paper again.'

'Oh, paint'll do. Try the silver enamel.' Pickup thought it politic to add, 'the stream looks awfully realistic.'

After the moat only the wire fence remained, which they'd already agreed could only be suggested, not reproduced in detail. Pickup had suggested the uprights – old gramophone needles from the radiogram downstairs, tapped in an inch apart and painted grey. Now Stanley would link them up with one, two if possible, strands of 2-amp fuse wire. He unwound the loose end from the card and kneeling low, putting his blotchy face close to the model, painfully anchored it to the nearest upright.

From downstairs Pickup's mother called that there was a cup of tea if they would like it. Pickup shouted back that they would. He didn't much like tea but it made a cigarette taste nice. Stanley looked up when he heard a sound on the stairs and said, 'Aren't you going to go down, Michael?'

Pickup said, 'She'll bring it.' The sketch

15

plan and fuzzy oblique photographs and the big working plan he and Stanley had constructed in Indian ink on tracing paper – Stanley doing the drawing, he providing some dubious expertise on aerial survey from the Tripos course – lay on the floor. He kicked them under the bed out of sight as his mother came in. She had her hat on still and a Craven A hanging from her lips. She carried a tray on which were two cups, the silver sugar bowl and tongs and some petit beurres. Stanley scrambled clumsily to his feet to take the tray.

'How very kind of you, Mrs. Pickup.'

She peered absent-mindedly through the smoke of her cigarette at the model. 'That *is* nice. What is it again?'

Stanley said, 'I'm really not very sure, Mrs. Pickup. Michael's being rather secretive about it.'

'I'm *not*. I told you, it's a vacation exercise; that's all, very boring.'

His mother, who wasn't really interested, smiled brightly at Stanley and changed the subject. 'Is there going to be a war?'

'We hope and pray not, Mrs. Pickup.'

'It's dreadful, isn't it?' She hadn't listened to his answer. 'I expect your mother is very worried.'

16

'What mother isn't?' asked Stanley sententiously.

'Mr. Pickup said he passed a queue of people in Birkenhead waiting for their gas-masks and standing there were lots of young men of nineteen or twenty who would be called up the minute there was a war.' Pickup had laughed dutifully at his father's scathing tones – 'soft twerps,' he had added – while remembering what his father seemed to forget, if never his mother, that he was nineteen himself within a couple of months and though students were deferred from conscription at present (and rightly: who wanted to be a silly militiaman?) there was no guarantee that they would still be if war did come. Anyway he was definitely going to join the University Air Squadron this year, especially if Nick Amering did.

Stanley was replying with his usual bloody painful sincerity and his mother probably wasn't listening, she never did. It was hardly very tactful of her to raise the subject since Stanley was twenty, and therefore even more call-upable, and what's more, Pickup suspected, was going to register as a conchie. He looked out of the window again at the sandhills, where two poor kids, a boy whose thick, flapping shorts reached below his knees, and a little lank-haired girl whose dirty knickers drooped below her frock, played at sliding down a sand-slope: through their shouts he could hear the plonk of ball on composition and occasional well-bred feminine cry from the tennis court of the Bayliss's house the far side of the sandhills and hidden from view by the tallest dune. Deep inside him he felt a sudden certainty that this hot, still September weekend which already seemed to have lasted for ever, was not the end of the world, that within a few days everything would be As It Had Been, he would go back to Cambridge and then perhaps would have to go through with – and again there came that nasty little clammy spasm down in his bowels.

His mother was saying, 'To think Michael was only in Germany two months ago. He hasn't told us much about what he did there.'

'I did. I told you lots.'

'Did you, dear?' she said vaguely, and to Stanley again, darting off again, 'I think Mr. Chamberlain's wonderful, don't you? Going on all these long journeys in an aeroplane at his age.'

'Michael thinks he should have gone in a British one.'

'It wasn't anything, just something to say.'

18

He hated people repeating what he'd said to other people like that, Stanley was always doing it; but his mother only shook her head disapprovingly and said that it was wicked, all this flying, wicked. He listened to her footsteps as she went away, sharp on the lino of the landing, muffled on the staircarpet, and remembered for no reason the times he'd been in bed with measles, mumps, chickenpox, colds, coughs, and had charted the course of the day by distant reverberations of her steps, hoping always for the pressure on the stairs and then the click-clack approach that meant something to eat or drink or a magazine brought back from the shops.

Stanley drank his tea with the exaggerated satisfaction he must have copied from his mother, and bent himself to the fiddly job of stringing the fuse wire. His big hairy fingers were extraordinarily deft. He said, 'I must say it would be a help if we knew what it was all supposed to be.'

Pickup said irritably. 'I told you, the whole point is that we don't. It's an exercise in interpreting from aerial survey.'

'Well, of course, if it helps you with your results, Michael, it'll be time well spent indeed.'

19

'I'd have made a mess of it without you.' He looked through the window to the scruffy dun-coloured slopes and coarse grass hillocks of the sandhills across which, as a boy, he'd come fleeing home from pursuing Bucks, though each year more aware of – and grateful for – the bungalows and Sunshine Villas which encroached reassuringly on the wilderness until now only a narrow, house-locked strip remained and the white-washed fisherman's cottage which even last year had still been inhabited by an aboriginal fisher family was finally an untidy ruin smelling of pee–

'When is the exam again?'

'Thursday.' It hadn't actually occurred to Pickup to pretend the model was part of the Mechanical Sciences Qualifying he had to re-sit before his second year. Stanley had jumped to that conclusion himself. Well, it all helped.

Stanley said, 'Then this is your last week-end? Perhaps we might go to the cinema tonight?'

'Mmm,' said Pickup without enthusiasm. Stanley and Stanley's religion disapproved of the cinema. The offer must have represented great willingness on his part.

He was saved by the shrill ring of the telephone and a moment later his father calling up to him. The ritual slang greeting came in a jaunty voice that was for Pickup at this moment the most welcome in the world.

'Paddy! When did you get back? Your ma said it would be next month–'

'Oh, wars and rumours of wars. They brought us back in a panic, don't ask me why. Docked at Southampton and here I am.'

'Good-o.'

'A jar tonight? Or are you due to be holding hands, if not worse, with some scrubber on the back row of the Wints?'

'Three were looking forward to it but they'll have to go without.'

Upstairs again he said to Stanley, 'I'm sorry, I forgot. I already promised to go out with Paddy Hutton.'

'I thought he was at sea.'

'He got back early. Something to do with the Crisis.'

Stanley's glasses winked as he looked up for a second. 'Well of course you must keep your promise. I dare say mother would like me at home this evening, anyway, with the world in such a state.' He bent over the model. When he spoke next, without looking up, he began, 'Michael,' and Pickup knew what was coming.

'What?'

'It's a long time since we saw you at Christian Soldiers.'

Pickup grunted.

Stanley forged on. 'A lot of chaps lose touch when they leave home and go to university et cetera, it's very easy, I know. But it's surprising how many make the effort when they can. Last Sunday we had – oh, six or seven you'd know: Beeston, Storey, Jones, O.H...'

Pickup listened to the names with stony indifference, but he said, 'All right, I'll try.'

Stanley sat back and looked critically at his handiwork.

The model was finished: a rectangle, four feet long and eighteen inches wide, enclosed by a half-inch wall, inside that the fence and tiny painted moat. The broader silver paper stream ran only on one side. At the corners, and at intermediate points along the sides, were towers cut from quarter-inch balsa, each topped with a tiny pyramidal roof. Inside, the two rows of long huts; between them, the road lined with inch-high poplars which Stanley had fashioned in loving detail from wire and cotton wool and green ink. At one end was the open space or parade ground which Pickup thought was the most realistic bit of all. Stanley had smeared on glue, then they'd sprinkled the glue with sand from the sandhills and blown away the excess. Beyond this space was the bigger, higher building whose long wings seemed to threaten the rest of the layout like the arms of a wrestler poised for combat.

Stanley peered at the photograph again. He said for the umpteenth time, 'We can't be sure this is exactly how the big building will look. It's only under construction in the photographs. But judging by the scaffolding and the bit they have got up–'

'It doesn't matter,' said Pickup impatiently. He corrected himself. 'It's super, honestly. Just what I wanted.'

Stanley said, 'How will you get it all that way? It'll want careful packing.'

'Mum'll do it. She's very good at doing up parcels.' Now it was finished he was anxious only, ungratefully, to smuggle Stanley out before his mother thought of asking him to stay to supper or something awful like that. Faintly, he heard the sudden voice below which, momentarily loud, then muted again, more even and insistent than any ordinary human voice, meant his father had switched on the wireless. It would be nearly six o'clock, time for the news. He said, 'I'll walk along the Prom with you if you're going that way. I promised I'd take the dog.' As they went downstairs and he unhooked the red leather lead from the cloakroom and the dog leaped and wagged in extravagant anticipation and Stanley called obsequious goodbyes, the pips were sounding.

The passengers spilled untidily from the boat train that had just crept, late and crowded, into Victoria. Many were holiday-makers, red-necked, irritable, unsure whether they had done right to cut short their holidays this crisis weekend. Others had closed homes in Rapallo, Deauville or Baden Baden, and their boxes and trunks and wheelchairs and even pictures wrapped in sacking accumulated in heaps on the platform while porters and taxis were whistled up. Among those who stood waiting to greet the homecomers were a grey-haired man who sported a rose in the button-hole of his plaid suit and a small, dumpy woman who diffidently held before her a crayoned notice saying REFUGEES AID. They studied the flow of passengers anxiously. Twice they began to move towards one of them, only to fall back again. Then the woman said with certainty, 'There he is.' A

24

gaunt figure had emerged from the rearmost coach and was moving hesitantly towards them. Even in the heat of the station he wore a dark overcoat reaching foreignly to his ankles and a hat pulled low on his bony brown head.

The pair advanced towards him, the woman holding her placard out to catch his eye. He looked at it, looked past them. The man with the buttonhole cleared his throat. The woman smiled nervously and uttered a name. The gaunt man stopped and put down the small suitcase that was all he carried. The woman smiled again, more confidently, and spoke a few words of German, if with little attempt at a German accent. He listened carefully and nodded. The man with the button-hole preferred English. He spoke slowly and loudly. As they turned to take the exit into Wilton Road he was saying, 'We have found you a room – you understand *room* – just to be going on with, and we hope you'll be very comfortable, but if it's *not* suitable the office is open on Monday again and they'll soon have you fixed up somewhere.'

Paddy Hutton was in fact only a few weeks older than Pickup but had always seemed more grown-up, more assured. The assurance still obtained, Pickup acknowledged as he strove to attract the attention of the slow-motion waiter, or potman, or whatever he was, who worked in the back bar of the Lodge on crowded, smoky Saturday nights, but after three terms of Cambridge he was suddenly, rather shamefully, aware of an outlook as narrow, in its way, as Stanley's. Paddy had been two years a Merchant Navy apprentice, had been to Lagos and Durban and Oran and Aden and Port Said, about which there was a hot book in the public library *(Boy* by James Hanley) and yet his horizons still seemed limited to those of the Urban District. He was looking forward to the end of his indentures when he would come home again for six months to study for his third mate's ticket, taking the train every day into Liverpool like Geoff Taylor or Garwood, who worked in banks, or Brian Mickle in the dried fruit business. He was good-looking in all the ways Pickup would have liked to have been and wasn't: medium height instead of being long and skinny, dark straight hair instead of frizzy mouse, complexion seasoned by sun and salt. Half the girls around had had crushes on him at one time or another. He had an aunt who'd married a German and in 1936, the Olympics year, he'd spent a long summer holiday there, coming back with enthusiastic stories and a red Swastika for his bike.

'It would be nuts having a war against Germany,' he was saying. 'Honestly, they're just like us only more organized – but you've been there now, you know what I mean.'

'Yes, well,' Pickup began, but Paddy hadn't finished.

'Against the Russians, certainly, or the lousy French – their customs came on at Oran and turned us inside-bloody-out and all for nothing, just for the sake of it.' He took a fat ship's Woodbine from the packet in front of him and pushed them towards Pickup. 'Though if there's going to be a war at all I'd sooner it waited a year. When I get my ticket' – he rolled his eyes in mock-doubt – '*if* I get it, I go straight into the R.N.R. as a sub-lieutenant. What about you? Have you joined anything?' – since the crisis started there'd been a wave of joining up, the local territorial regiment, or the balloon barrage in Liverpool, or the A.R.P., or for some of the yachtsmen a mysterious auxiliary unit that was only referred to in whispers.

'I thought I'd join the air squadron when I

27

get back to Cambridge.'

'Mmm.' Paddy nodded his head solemnly. 'Do they fly?'

'Only Tiger Moths.'

'Well, these little stunt planes I saw at Bochum that time, they were only like Tiger Moths, except for stubby wings, and I never saw such flying – there wasn't a thing they didn't do with them!'

As he contrived at last to catch the waiter's eye, and as Paddy enlarged for the umpteenth time on the air display he'd seen in 1936, Pickup briefly faced the truth that he'd outgrown Paddy Hutton, too. Though in a way he preferred, or at least was more relaxed, in their company he couldn't help measuring his old cronies against Amering and Nicholson and Linné, and finding them – well, unsurprising and what was worse, unsurprisable. He and Paddy would sit and drink tonight and probably get involved sooner or later with the rest of the crowd, and there'd be a few stories and a few dirty jokes, all acquired somewhere else and doggedly passed on, but no wit, no instant, improvised, accumulative fantasy of the sort which Amering – usually – would start and the rest of you take up; no finding ideas as ludicrous as lavatories or beds; no impulsive jokes like the time they'd drifted for no reason into the tea dance at the Dorothy Café and improvised (in unnaturally loud voices but with jolly straight faces) a tense scene of the sort you got in stupid Bulldog Drummond, full of cries of 'You don't mean? – not Phyllis?' to the embarrassed fascination of the earth-people around; no more deliberate stunts like the Loch Ness monster they'd rigged up, which successfully navigated the Cam from Magdalene Bridge to Queens' and was photographed and appeared in the *Daily Graphic* with the headline *'Monster' Was Student Hoax*, or now the one (and that cold blink inside again) that they'd hatched–

'So you've been in Germany now?' Paddy was saying, still with his serious look. 'I got your postcard finally when we docked the day before yesterday.'

'It was a kind of tour – I mean we went down through France to Switzerland and Austria and came back through das Reich. This friend of mine Nick Amering–'

'Friend from the university?'

'Sort of. There's three or four of us knock around together. Nick – Nick Amering, that is – and Ian Nicholson, who sometimes gets called Nick, too, which is confusing, and

Philipp Linné who's a German, really, though they live in Switzerland – they're the Linné in Beaton-Linné, you know the electric trains and turbines firm – at least his father does. His mother's in London, I think they're divorced or something.' He didn't mention, because he didn't want to brag to Paddy, the Linné's château where they'd stayed which was more like a hotel, only better, and wondered, in the same mood of diffidence, whether to – how to – go on to the thing about those hot, bright days and long roads and scarlet banners and scents of flowers that he'd most looked forward to revealing but when the time came shrank back for fear the telling would dissipate the wonder, the incredulity even, which he'd managed to keep intact even after two months. He said as casually as he could, 'Then there was this sister of Nick's we brought back with us.'

'Hullo, hullo, hullo. Dark horse Pickup. Tell me more' – and worse than that, tell *us* more, because some others of the crowd had arrived from somewhere, Dicker Brown and Pat Rogers and Schofield, and Paddy was saying what about the dark horse then, abroad with a girl? No, it was nothing like that, after all her brother was there, too. Oh,

Jill she was called, about seventeen or eighteen (as if he didn't know to the day), she was studying in Munich (he could hardly use the term which the Amerings used themselves, which was 'finishing off'). They'd brought her back for the summer holidays ... but as he hesitated before taking the big plunge attention was abruptly switched from him.

'Christ,' said Paddy, 'I forgot.' He slapped his breast theatrically on the bulge of the wallet in his inside pocket. 'Talking of girls, talking of GIRLS' – the wallet was out now and he was thumbing through the compressed wodge of letters and forms and foreign money. He found a snapshot, glossy and deckle-edged like they did them abroad, and handed it to Schofield on the other side from Pickup, Pickup only getting a half glimpse, without actually seeing anything somehow knowing what it would be. Paddy said, 'Chap I know in the Garden Line took it from the deck in Barcelona.'

Schofield whistled and showed Pat Rogers. Pickup felt excitement and curiosity and nervousness, too. He craned his head as Rogers passed the snap to Dicker Brown. The girl was standing in the stern of a rowing boat, looking up in the direction of the photographer, the last thing she'd taken off –

knickers, or perhaps a petticoat – trailed from her hand across the gunwale, but it was the black triangle of her hair that took his stare, that he'd never seen before in a nude photograph– 'Apparently they row out to where you're anchored and strip for money – or better still, food. You know, the blockade and all that, You throw it down to them. These two did it for– Oh Christ, I don't remember exactly: something like a couple of loaves of bread and some coffee and sugar and a tin of milk. They're not just pros, like, but decent girls – that's the whole point.'

'Which side are they on?' said Dicker Brown.

'The port's held by the Reds. But whether the judies are Reds or not I wouldn't know. Or care.'

'They're all alike stripped off,' said Dicker, and the others laughed. Pickup peered over his shoulder with mock deliberation, 'Not bad, not bad. A hundredth at f. 5.6, I'd say, light yellow filter.' At last he held the snap for himself.

The second girl had been doing the rowing. She was sitting with her back to the camera, still undressing, only her top off, fumbling with the fasteners of her skirt or something. If the picture could have been taken a minute later – he studied the other one again, avidly. What bothered him was how she stood, how she held the last garment, whatever it was, away from her body, not trying to hide anything, and – sharp, unmistakable even in the 6 by 9 cm. print – the look in her eyes: bold and laughing and yet ... well, rueful.

'I'll tell you one thing,' said Paddy, 'they haven't got a chance. Franco's going to win, thank God!' There was a murmur of approval.

The gaunt man came to a little street market, not more than twenty stalls but still brightly lit this late Saturday evening, mostly by electricity, one or two still by naphtha lanterns which particularly seemed to affect him, for he stood and stared at them for some minutes. Then he studied the saveloys and pies and salt beef of the cooked meat stall, putting his head close to read the price tickets until the stallkeeper, not wanting a vagrant breathing over his perishables, spoke harshly and the gaunt man, blinking, moved away.

He re-entered the narrow street by which he had come to the market. There was a butcher's shop still open, the butcher a big man in a blue and white apron who held aloft cuts of meat as he recommended them in a loud voice, knocking pennies – even sixpence sometimes – off the price in order to clear as many as possible before he closed, and the shoppers, who knew this custom and had waited until the last hour, got their Sunday joint at what they hoped were bargain prices. So much the gaunt man, in his myopic way, had deduced. But now his mind was made up and he hurried to the eel shop he had passed earlier, outside whose entrance he had hovered, noting the procedure, the money needed. For tenpence he got a thick white bowl of stewed eels, a scoop of mashed potato and ladleful of unnaturally green parsley sauce, a slice of bread and butter. He ate hungrily but carefully, cleaning all the flesh off the little circlets of spine before laying them aside. On the next marble-topped table he noticed that some previous diner had left almost untouched his slice of bread. He watched it anxiously until, pretending to reach for the stone jar of salt, he could gather it up, fold it, and slip into the pocket of his long overcoat.

But after the pub had closed and the crowd had broken into ones and twos and gone different ways, he and Paddy walked back along the Prom, past both their corners until in turn the Sunshine Villas and the older, rather more imposing houses finally petered out and there was only the shabby concrete seawall and the scrubland behind. The tide was up, bringing with it a fresh breeze. Pickup felt comfortable, loquaciously full of beer, with no sickness threatening at all. The photograph was, for the moment, dormant. When they'd left behind the last of the lovers who murmured to each other enfolded in each other's arms they stopped and peed ten feet down into the sea.

'Christ, doesn't that German beer go through you?' said Paddy.

'In Munich we drank five steins each one night,' Pickup bragged. 'That's over nine pints. The only trouble was we got taken short trying to get to the hotel. We were absolutely desperate for–' He stopped, remembering something.

'Don't say you went in the *strasse*. The Germans wouldn't think that very funny.'

'No, we found a place open. In the station.' He stopped short again.

Paddy, not noticing, said, 'It packs a wallop, too. The first time Heinrich took me out – that's my aunty's husband – I got so squiffed he had to take me home. Well, almost *carry* me. All his pals were laughing and slapping me on the back but there was nothing spiteful about them. Nice guys. And a marvellous place. You know, so clean and everyone proud of it. Honestly, Micky, didn't you feel that it was a country that – that knows where it's going? I'm so fed up with these crummy newspapers that are always on about Hitler as if he were some tyrant or something.'

'We only have the *Mail* at home, and they're pretty well for him, actually.'

'Mum gets the *News Chronicle,* being a Methodist, and every day it's got some niggle about the Jews or someone. I wish someone would do something about our Jew-boys.'

Pickup was silent, The only Jew he knew for certain was a Jew was Sarah Friedlander who was Christopher Bright's girlfriend in S.12 just across the landing from him in college.

'Great greasy yids,' said Paddy. 'When they go in at the Baths – if they ever go in – you can see the grease floating on the water after them.' He buttoned his fly and slapped his pockets to find the bulge of his cigarettes. 'They say the hotels in Llandudno

36

have been chock full of them ever since the crisis started. In case Liverpool or Manchester get bombed!'

Pickup made a tiny snort but he didn't feel either amused or derisive. The possibility of air-raids had been a secret nightmare ever since the one in *Things to Come* when Raymond Massey and the others had strolled out into the snowy evening after their Christmas party, with Christmassy music still playing, and then had looked up, suddenly aghast, at the sound of many motors high in the sky above. He said, 'Paddy, that time I was telling you about, in Munich when we'd had all that beer. It was about two o'clock in the morning – we'd been on to a sort of night-club–'

'Aye-aye then? Night-clubs too?'

'It wasn't one with girls. I mean, not dancers or anything. Mostly talking – it was supposed to be satirical or something. I didn't understand much of it. Anyway, we were walking back and desperate for a slash and Nick or someone remembered the station. There was no one about much and it was all sort of closed off and no one being allowed in except for people going to catch a night sleeper. We were talking English and they must have thought we were going, too, and we went through and then coming away there's a subway thing that joins the main station with the one for local trains, the Starnberger they call it, and suddenly we saw these men ... there must have been a hundred of them at least – with bald heads and their clothes kind of flapping on them, and chains – all chained together – and guards shouting at them, and at us too – to go away.'

Paddy drew on his cigarette. 'You don't believe all those stories, do you?'

Pickup wailed, 'But we saw these people. We *saw* them.'

The room contained iron bed, bedside table with Bible, wardrobe, chair, gasfire, wash-stand with basin and ewer, and on the floor a strip of old stair carpet. The only light was from a hanging 40 watt bulb. Still in his long overcoat the gaunt man picked up the Bible. He held it very close to his nose, only inches away, but after a few moments lowered it again and rubbed his eyes in the manner – finger on one, thumb on the other, finally closing on the bridge of the nose – of all those who wear glasses. He took off the long coat, laid it on the bed and began to undress.

Christian Soldiers was held in the big room of the pious prep school to which Pickup, and most of his friends in the Urban District, had gone as dayboys. There were also boarders for whom attendance was compulsory, who therefore filled up most of the seats, boily necks above Sunday Eton collars, exuding that remembered boarder smell of porridge and floor polish and stale fart. The rest of the assembly was made up from current day boys, the old boys Stanley named plus a couple more – they all looked at Pickup with exaggerated surprise – and the usual masters and headmaster's family. Stanley was standing up in front, Bible in hand, spotty red face to one side, subject: Talking Things Over with Jesus, not just praying for things but sharing all your thought with Him. Pickup shifting position on the hard chair, thought with a defiant detachment that the last thing he wanted to do was to share his thoughts, especially when that girl in the rowing boat kept filling them.

Not that there weren't distant (though ever less distant) apprehensions that he wished he could control as once he had been able to control, by fierce prayer, the dread of threatened vengeance by Bucks or at this school of singing lessons or at the grammar school of gym–

People were scuffling to their feet for a chorus. Mrs. William, the headmaster's brother William's wife, thumped at the piano.

*A little talk with Jesus*
*Makes it right, all right...*

Equally there were things to be looked forward to, to be prayed *for*, not prayed against. At Sunday dinner his mother had returned to the proposed weekend at Nick's between the exam and the beginning of Full Term, over which she'd been brooding ever since the word CRISIS – this morning supplanted in the headlines of the *Sunday Dispatch* by ULTIMATUM – had blown up.

'It would be madness to be in London at a time like this. I wouldn't have a moment's peace worrying about you.'

'But I've got to go back for the exam anyway, you know that.'

'To Cambridge, yes, if you really have to, and at a time like this you'd think they wouldn't worry about things like exams–'

'Oh *Ma* – for heaven's sake.'

'But Cambridge is at least in the country.

I'm not having you in London where the air-raids would be. You can come home again after the exam, then we'll see how things are when the term begins properly.'

'It's silly to come back all the way just for about five days, and a whole extra return fare–'

'Your father will pay that, won't you, George?'

There was nothing vague about her when she was after her own Way, Pickup had reflected. He'd said, 'Besides it's a proper invitation to stay with the Amerings, from Nick's mother. They may have fixed up some things.'

'No one would hold you to an invitation at a time like this. I doubt very much if they're still expecting you–'

'How do you know they're not?'

'I'll write to Mrs. Amering.'

'If you do I'll never speak to you again. Anyway, it's not Mrs. Amering, it's Lady Amering.'

His mother had blinked and Pickup had sensed that this surprising, to him rather embarrassing, item of information had disconcerted her as no argument could have done. She'd said, 'Well, it's up to your father. He's not to go, is he, George?'

41

His father had said, 'We'll see nearer the time.'

The chorus had finished. People sat down, then leaned forward in the jacknifed, bottom-protruding, head-buried-in-hands posture that was adopted – rather than actually kneeling – for prayer. Pickup closed his eyes and thought with relief that the service would soon be over. Stanley's voice rose and fell. Peace, an end to armament, that the leaders of men might turn away from the League of Nations and other worldly delusions and turn to God – the familiar catalogue of intercession unrolled: for Haskin, G.H. that his grievous illness might soon be lifted from him; for missionaries in the field, bringing the Good News to all who thirsted for it; for both teams in the housematch next week, that they might play their hardest, in the name of Jesus Christ Our Saviour... Why did it all have to be so 'umble, so cringing? It wasn't England that was threatening war, it was the other side. Nobody wanted a war. It would be ghastly and besides it would finally bonk the London weekend on the head, though on the other hand it would also remove that looming cloud–

Suddenly he was attentive. Stanley had

switched to something else, to those who were oppressed for their belief– 'And, O Lord, we think especially of our brethren in Germany who we have been told suffer imprisonment and great hardships because of bearing Witness for Thee. Comfort them, O Lord, and incline the heart of Herr Hitler, if it be Thy Will, that he may see the Light and throw open the gates, tear down the bars and join in singing Thy praises, Amen.' Pickup stared between his fingers at Stanley. Did he know? Did he suspect? But how could he? He was too wet. Besides, the person they had in mind wasn't in the least religious, by the sound of him; more like an atheist. It must be coincidence unless – and Pickup squinted up in even greater consternation – unless it were a SIGN. He squeezed his eyes shut and willed an urgent conversation heavenwards.

# CHAPTER 2

Pickup edged his way awkwardly out of Sloane Square underground. The model, though carefully packed by his mother in a shallow box of thick card covered in shiny green stuff cut down from an old – perhaps even pre-war – gown box and then wrapped in thick brown paper and tied with much knotted string, still made an awkward armful, especially as there was also the Revelation suitcase bought for the continental tour and much too big, really, for a weekend. But a taxi from Liverpool Street would have been unthinkable. The trouble was that it was now one o'clock and he wasn't sure what time the Amerings had their lunch. He didn't know if they were expecting him for lunch. To face the full truth he wasn't sure they were still expecting him at all. At his mother's nagging he had written to Nick to say, in as casual and jocular a manner as he could assume, that if things really did get worse he might have to dash home after the MSQE and help with the yobs from Liverpool that were going to be billeted on them, something like that. But Nick hadn't replied – perhaps he should have written to Lady Amering really – and though the news had got gloomier and gloomier, so that his mother had worked herself into a state even about his leaving for Cambridge on the Wednesday morning, that very afternoon old Chamberlain had announced that he and Hitler and Mussolini and everyone were going to meet in Munich the next day and by the time he'd reached Cambridge the evening paper headlines were for the first time optimistic. Through the pre-occupations of the exam on Thursday he'd sensed the relief that was waiting to come whistling out of everyone once that peace was official. Today it was.

The problem remained of what to do about the Amerings. Simply take a taxi from the rank at Sloane Square and bowl up? Or telephone first? He stared across at Peter Jones, clean and cubist and glass-walled, one of the new buildings, like Highpoint flats or the Cambridgeshire village colleges or the Liverpool Philharmonic Hall, which his books on modern architecture said it was proper to admire. Reaching a decision he pushed into a phone booth by the Royal

Court Theatre. The voice that answered was cool and clipped but also disconcerting. For some reason, to actually address someone as 'Lady' seemed outside his capability as well as outside his experience. He said lamely, 'Is that, er, Nick's mother?'

'Speaking.'

'This is Michael Pickup.'

'Oh, *hallo*. We weren't sure whether still to expect you.'

'I'm sorry, I should have—'

'No, no, how could anyone tell? Isn't it welcome news from Germany? Now where are you? – Liverpool Street?'

'No, actually I'm quite close – Sloane Square. I just stopped off to phone...' Too late he wished he'd said he was still the other side of London, for there was the shortest of pauses the other end before she replied.

'Oh, in that case do come straight on. We've just started lunch, I'm afraid, but only just.'

'If you're sure it's all right—'

'Of course it is. We'll expect you shortly.'

But it was another ten minutes before the taxi had delivered him to a tall corner house in a small private square off Old Church Street and a man in a linen jacket had opened the door with a look of what to Pickup seemed distaste and they'd wrestled briefly with the case and the parcel and Pickup had said No, he didn't need to wash his hands, aware too late that they were hot and sticky, and been propelled, red faced, into a dining-room where the hush on his entering was bad enough, not to mention the introductions and not knowing whether he ought to shake hands when they were occupied with some sort of fish, without finding Jill Amering sitting there with that wide teasing smile.

'I thought you'd be back with the vons and zus,' he said, realizing even as he said it that with the Crisis *of course* she wouldn't. What on earth had he been thinking–

'And get locked away for the duration if there'd been a war? God, no. Besides the poor lambs would have been too embarrassed. They don't know how to look me in the eye at the best of times'– the vons and zus was how everyone referred to the impoverished Munich family with whom she was being finished.

Lady Amering, who had clipped features to match her clipped voice and very brown hair and wore soft, floppy clothes that Pickup thought must be artistic, said, 'Next week, Jill dear, if it really is all over. The

47

poor things are really rather dependent on their girls.'

Jill gave the tiny habitual toss that Pickup remembered, as if tossing hair out of her eyes, though in fact her stiff, almost wiry, waves came nowhere near her eyes. 'I don't mind. Where are we? – end of September? Kurt and his crowd are always on about some great beer splurge they have about now. I said I'd drink pint for pint with them – gave the vons and zus a fit, they think beer's ungracious for a girl.' She mimicked. 'A glass of wine, Yilli, that is nicer, yes?'

There was a chuckle from a big peppery man, an uncle or possibly a grandfather; in the confusion of his arrival Pickup hadn't registered the exact relationship, only that he was General someone.

'Anyway,' said Jill, 'there's this stupefying party I'm supposed to give.'

'What party is that, Jilly dear?' said the aunt who went with the peppery general.

'Oh God, you will all have to be hostess at one sooner or later, on your birthday if you have one while you're there, otherwise some date they fix. You know, long white gloves and two glasses of fizz and a lot of terrible old trout and one Bavarian minister or something.'

'I must say it's very agreeable of the Frei-herr and seine Dame,' said Lady Amering.

'*You* pay for it, don't worry. Nick said he might whizz down for it – you will, won't you, Nick? For my sake.'

Nick said calmly, 'It depends. We might all come, mightn't we, Michael?'

Made the focus of attention again, Pickup choked over the salt, lukewarm soup the man in the linen jacket had brought him which he'd been gulping down as fast as was consistent with table manners, afraid that they'd all wait and watch until he caught up–

Fortunately, Lady Amering murmured that the General wanted to get to his bridge at the Club, would Michael think them very rude if they started the pudding? Jill, overhearing his passionate assent, said, 'Don't worry, there'll be enough left for you, Henry says he can cut it into smaller bits,' and though she got more frowns than laughs (Nick's and his own nervous one), and though he knew it was just her way, partly playful, partly barbed, mostly showing off, he still felt his cheeks burn again. Worse, as they finally left the dining-room they would have to bump into Henry, if that was the linen-jacketed man's name, about to struggle upstairs with the great

49

suitcase and the parcel. Jill said, 'Thank God, Michael remembered his hunting things. I was afraid he would forget.'

Pickup muttered, 'Nick, the box is you-know-what,' which turned out to be rather a good thing to mutter, for Nick became serious and secretive and arranged for it to be taken down to the basement. But when he'd been shown to a bedroom with a creaky floor covered with a faded pink-and-green carpet, and had washed his hands in the washbasin he filled from a jug standing in it and combed his hair, and was looking out of the window over a little sunless square of garden, he heard Jill's voice funnelling from kitchen regions, 'God, does that mean he'll have to come to the Verriers' with us?' – and then perhaps she was hushed because there were only low mutterings. Pickup re-examined the thought that had occurred to him ever since he was shown into the dining-room: that if he telephoned home they might still screech at him to come back, and, even if they didn't, it would be easy, by a hint of uncertainty or unease, to plant the idea. He began to compose a polished apology. 'So sorry, Lady Amering, but it seems I have to dash home after all. I've been helping an architect friend with a scheme and we've got to revise part of

50

it rather urgently. Another time? Of course, I'd love to...' At this moment Jill and Nick appeared in the little garden, poking among the dusty shrubs. Their heads were very close, his hand rested lightly on her shoulder. Pickup was bitten again by the fierce envy – jealousy, really – he'd felt at times on the Tour, of their closeness. He had no brother or sister himself. Jill bent down and extracted a tiny black kitten from behind a bush. Stroking it she suddenly looked up, saw Pickup before he could retreat and gave him a wide dazzling smile.

'Aren't you coming down?'

'Hang on.' He ran down the stairs.

In the store the air was heavy with a mixture of smells: vanilla, cheap scent, oilcloth and hot feet. The gaunt man picked his way slowly between the counters heaped with sweets and biscuits, past the ice-cream and toys and comics and stationery and electric fittings and trays and trays of screws until he came, wondering, to the spectacles. The counter was divided into many compartments, some containing lenses, others frames, others whole glasses. The gaunt man put his face close to a chart of instructions printed at the top in giant letters and below in ones that line by line diminished in size. After a while he began to try on spectacles. At first he put them on properly, hooking them over his ears before peering at the text. Later he just held them before his eyes, but continued to work methodically, replacing each pair exactly where he had found it. The woman in maroon overall and frilly cap behind the counter surveyed him incuriously. At last the gaunt man seemed satisfied. He held a pair of spectacles in each hand, comparing them. He made his choice and offered the woman a sixpence which he had ready in his pocket. She stared and said, brusquely at first, then loudly and slowly, as if to a child, 'No, it's sixpence each piece, the frame and the two lenses, you need one-and-six.' Shaking his head vexedly the gaunt man sought the additional shilling.

The screen was tiny and bulbous and spotted, like a snowstorm in a glass ball. Pickup was still astonished. He knew about television, along with all the other marvels of the future, from the magazines he'd read as a boy oh years before but had never realized that it had actually arrived or that people, even people like the Amerings, had sets in their homes. Sir Talbot had come home with the evening paper and shouted excitedly for everyone to come and view, which was helpful for Pickup because his meeting with Nick's father was consequently rushed and informal, without feeling all eyes were on him. Sir Talbot was an enthusiast for all things electrical and mechanical. He said, 'This is a moment of history for broadcasting, a moment of history.'

At present, though, the picture was of an empty field. The voice of the commentator came again, very clear and near compared with the wireless, almost as if he were in the upstairs drawing-room with them, saying that all eyes were turned to the sky but still no sign of the machine. Then they were looking at a little group waiting on the tarmac, all rather dark and indistinct except for the lofty outline of a top hat. The commentator was identifying the members when with some excitement he broke off and they were back on the field and amongst the dots of light was a darker dot in the sky, getting bigger. Pickup leaned forward as the Lockheed touched down and taxied towards the tarmac. As it stopped they must have changed to another camera, for the viewpoint was now much closer. Pickup caught a glimpse of the pilot's face framed by his side-window, then they were focused expectantly on the door of the plane as mechanics manoeuvred the steps into position. Someone from the welcoming group was coming forward; the door half-opened, stayed so for an instant, was finally thrust wide and there – moving, animated – were the wing-collar and scrawny neck and striped trousers that had figured on every front page for the past week. In his hand the Prime Minister held a piece of paper. As he began to speak the camera seemed to be trying to crane closer and closer. Applause and some cheers broke out from the crowd. The commentator whispered, 'Yes, I think you'll be able to see it now – there on the paper – Herr Hitler's signature, and that of Mr. Chamberlain...'

Shamefully, but in the darkened room not disastrously, Pickup became aware of smarting eyes, of indefinable emotion welling up as it had used to do at the pictures, predictably when the V.C. was hung on the dead officer's horse in *Lives of a Bengal lancer,* for instance, or quite inexplicably when the eclipse had come in the nick of time to save them all in *King Solomon's Mines.*

Nicholson and Linné had arrived noisily in Nicholson's Morgan. They went down to Nick's den, white-tiled like a lavatory, lit only by a high little window behind a grating. It had been used for a long time as a darkroom and still smelled of hypo, but there'd been some attempt to make it more sociable with painted cane chairs, cushions, and magazine pictures fixed to the wall with passe-partout tape. The model was unpacked on the table and really looked very impressive. Ian Nicholson crouched to bring his eyes on the same level, squinting down the poplar-lined thoroughfare. His expression was the hard, competitive expression that he wore whenever any challenge presented itself, whether it was shove-ha'penny in a Cambridgeshire pub or plane-tabling on the Gog and Magog hills – he had had to excel, Pickup thought, couldn't bear to be second. Philipp Linné also gazed with peculiar concentration. Nick, pouring gins and orange from a private supply, had to repeat his name before he blinked and took the proffered glass. 'Never known any of you need to be asked twice before.'

Linné shrugged and said, 'Don't forget, for me it is rather more ... personal. My fellow countrymen build it. The family business, or a branch of it, installs the generator.' His manicured finger rested lightly, momentarily, on one of the strands of fuse-wire.

There was only a faint trace of accent, nor did his floppy dark hair and handsome, straight-nosed face – the very kind of face that Pickup gave himself in his private dreams – look in any way German. Now Nicholson, he could have been the Hun in any of the stories that Pickup had been brought up on, with his stern square head and fair hair and brusque Wellington voice. But Linné was the one who was indefinably, unmistakably foreign. There was something more worldly, more adult: the smell of cologne and small cigars should have been about his head; in the showers he would have more body hair in more places; he alone, if the truth were admitted, would have been with a woman. By his side even Nick Amering looked a bit raw-boned and red-faced. Well, of course, Nick was such an odd mixture; built like a hearty, loud as a hearty but positively non-hearty; dressed always with an elegance that Pickup tried unsuccessfully to copy yet no aesthete; then this way of swinging every joke against himself rather than against other people, the way everyone liked him, and the way he was at his ease in any company–

Nicholson was asking, 'What's the scale, Mickup?'

'About an eight-hundredth. So every-thing's much too high. I mean, the trees should only be half an inch, really. But the lengths and breadths and distances are about right.'

Nicholson nodded. Philipp Linné lit a cigarette in an amber holder. 'War, it seems, having been averted for the moment–'

'Postponed,' said Nicholson.

'Bought off,' said Linné. 'Did you see the old fool waving his piece of paper?'

'Oh, I don't know. Mickup was quite moved by it, weren't you, Mickup?'

'I wasn't,' he protested angrily.

'Well, it *was* quite a moment,' said Nick judicially, though whether in his defence or of the television installation Pickup couldn't be sure.

'Anyway, the war being off, the rag, I take it, is now officially on?'

No one answered.

'The only thing is that in the presence of this model "rag" is manifestly not the word. This place is not Girton College. This place would be about as easy to penetrate – and to escape from again – as hell.' An alien, per-haps deliberate inflection on the last word made hell sound foreign, real and menacing.

'We hardly planned to take it by storm,'

said Nick.

'Some sort of ruse was the idea,' chipped in Pickup.

'Such as?'

'Visiting journalists. Or student-admirers of the regime. There was Nick's scheme to found a Cambridge University National Socialist Society–'

'*Cunns* for short,' said Nick with a grin, not at the joke itself. Pickup knew, but at the very idea of trying to swing it on the Proctors.

He said, 'We'd get write-ups in the papers.'

'The Progs would never allow it,' said Nicholson.

'Even better write-ups in the papers. The Germans would be bound to hear of it. We'd ask someone down from the Embassy, wangle a return invitation–'

'You're just playing,' said Linné sharply. 'The man who made this model possible, who took the photographs – he wasn't playing. He was taking his life in his hands, believe me.'

'*Helmuth?*' said Nick, He laughed in the boisterous, scoffing way he had sometimes had. 'Helmuth's all right. He's been bombarding Jilly with postcards from the Bodensee.'

'Besides, it is *his* friend we're trying to save.' Pickup could have bitten off his tongue. That was the kind of sneery remark that wasn't made – but Linné was sweeping on before anyone could pick it up.

'Whatever risk he did or did not run, what we have to do is to take maximum advantage of the result – and of Michael here's skill in translating it into shape.'

'A friend of mine helped a lot,' said Pickup modestly.

'You told him nothing? Of course you did not. So, we must bring the model to life. We must learn what every part does, where is the sick-bay, where the stores, where the kitchens–' he paused fractionally– 'and where is housed the turbine installed by the loyal firm of Bayerische Beaton Linné AG. We must learn which barracks are occupied by which categories of captive.'

'How?'

'We must find someone who knows the place, someone who has been imprisoned there. Every day now refugees from the Nazis arrive in this country. Among them must surely be one or two who have been in the camp. We must go to the organisations that bring in these refugees, the Quakers, the Jews–'

59

Nick said, 'My godmother's on some committee. I could try her.'

'Excellent. We should only have thought of it earlier. As for our strategy, it's obvious – we must take advantage of the accident that BBL put in the electrical generator. It's an entrée too good to neglect.'

Pickup asked, 'But have *we* the entrée to BBL?'

'Of course we have. My father may choose to live in Switzerland but he still cracks the whip over the affiliated companies. The day Ian and I took a look over the plant they couldn't do enough for us – you should have come as well, Mickup. It was quite interesting.'

Mickup was the nickname compounded from Mick and Pickup which Nicholson had invented, which luckily hadn't caught on with the others except – it had struck Pickup – when he was out of favour. He said, 'As a matter of fact it was the day Nick and Jill and I went swimming at you-know-where, which wasn't exactly a waste of time.' He had a sudden vivid memory of the crunch of gravel on the trim pathways leading to the river, the smell of lilac, quietness – almost a hush – the toytown houses with steep roofs and bright-painted woodwork, and recollection racing and jumping ahead like a film to the bathing place and Jill–

Linné said, 'It's a big one, too, the generator. Five thousand kilowatt, which is a lot to light a few searchlights. According to all the rumours the barbed wire is electrified.' Again he laid his finger lightly on the fuse-wire strands of the model.

'I told you, we could see the insulators.'

'Oh yes. I wonder if my father knows.' He shrugged. 'I would not mind betting he does. Anyway, the point is, of course, that as Bayerische Beaton Linné installed the plant they must also service it.'

'Does that follow?'

'Nearly always. Besides, I asked that fool of a manager, Ristow, just to embarrass him. He changed the subject but I saw him shoot a very guilty look at his precious files!' Linné lit another cigarette and flicked the spent match across the model; it came to rest in the middle of the sanded square. 'What more natural, more unsuspicious than a routine visit from a couple of maintenance men armed with the proper passes?'

'And who leave again smuggling someone out?' asked Nick.

'Perhaps. But rather risky, eh? Since the electrified wire and the searchlights are there to prevent escapes, suppose the power were to be cut off at a pre-arranged moment ... the someone could be waiting. It would be up to him.'

'A time-bomb, you mean?'

'Something like that.'

The tram squeaked and shuddered from the sunlight of the Embankment into the gloom of the Kingsway tunnel. From the upper deck the gaunt man stared at the blank walls without either greater or less attention than he had spared for the Thames, or the shipping on it, or the three sightseers who, this early October day, the Crisis only just past, gazed at Cleopatra's Needle. As the tram surfaced again he prepared to descend. Alighting at the Holborn fare stage he threaded his way through into Bloomsbury, stopping and frowning several times at street names, once having to retrace the way he had taken. Presently he came to a wide square whose houses were now mostly converted to offices. The gaunt man climbed the two broad steps to the front door of the most imposing building. Inside, the high-ceilinged entrance hall was crammed with chairs, even an old school bench, on which perhaps a score of men and women and children were waiting. From rooms off the hallway, and from up the wide staircase, came sounds of low conversation, the unnaturally loud clatter of a typewriter, once the ringing of a telephone, promptly answered. A woman behind a small table in one corner of the hall beckoned to the gaunt man, reaching for the letter he held up in front of him in the attitude of one long accustomed to the demands of bureaucracy.

The woman nodded her head over the note several times, then rustled importantly into one of the side rooms. Returning she motioned the gaunt man to wait on one of the vacant seats. He sat for perhaps half an hour, hands thrust into the pockets of the long coat, hat on head, before there was the sound of a car drawing up outside. The woman behind the table nodded deferentially to the first of the two young men who entered, and who presently addressed the gaunt man in German. The man rose to his feet and bowed. After a moment's hesitation they shook hands. The young man looked around the crowded hall and conferred briefly with his companion who, drawn into the encounter, now also extended his hand. He made a suggestion in less fluent German. The gaunt man inclined his head in agreement. The two young men led him out into the sunlight.

For Pickup, squeezing into the corner of the rear seat of the Lanchester to make room for Philipp Linné as well as Ian Nicholson, so that the stranger could go in the front, the first impression was of the foreignness of his hat: deep-crowned, dingy, seemingly too large for the bony head beneath; the second was his smell, which was musty and sour and also alien. Nick drove to an A.B.C. in Covent Garden where they found a table in an obscure corner. Still awash with lunchtime beer from the Anglesea free house Pickup sat over his coffee until it was lukewarm and scummy but the man, persuaded by Linné had a poached egg on toast followed by a chocolate biscuit. Linné spoke in a low voice, hesitantly, periodically pausing as if for confirmation of what he said. The man answered at first only in monosyllables; later he expanded slightly. At something Linné said he shook his head vehemently. Pickup became obsessed by his eyes which seemed clouded and painful so that the man blinked repetitively and once rubbed them.

They drove on again, through St. James's Park and Belgravia, to Old Church Street.

Nick got out first and made sure the way down to the basement was clear before beckoning to them. He heard Linné whispering cautiously as they entered the hall, but affected perhaps by the carpet on the floor or the Canaletto on the wall or the silver tray on the console table, the man hung back, holding his hand to his hat before finally, for the first time removing it. Pickup giggled in embarrassment. Nicholson mouthed fiercely at him. The man's head was covered with grey hair at most an inch long which sprouted patchily from the bony cranium. In the den they spread round the table. Pickup lifted the box lid from the model. The man stared at it without speaking.

Linné began his questions again, consulting a piece of paper in one hand, stabbing a finger of the other at the model as he sought to establish the name and function of each part. Pickup tried listening attentively but his German was confined to a few phrases remembered from the summer trip. Nicholson had school German only. Nick's wasn't bad but academic compared with Jill's, for instance. In her quick actressy way she had acquired a fluent apparently idiomatic command of the language after six months with the vons and zus.

Linné came to the end of his list and they all began to put questions, Linné interpreting for Nicholson and Pickup – the once Pickup got a word in – though again you couldn't be sure he wasn't skimping the job one way or the other if he himself thought the subject unimportant. Nicholson switched to his school Deutsch, numbering the questions in his harsh Wellington way, *ein, zwei, drei, vier.* The man became increasingly agitated. He pointed again and again at the drawbridge and covered gate and Pickup recognised some of the words he repeated each time more insistently – *nimmer* meaning never, and *verstehen* meaning understand, and of course, like a cough, like an old man clearing his throat, the name of the straggling little town into which they had ventured that summer's day–

'*Shssssh.*' Nick had his fingers to his lips. He opened the door a crack and peered out.

'What is is?' said Nicholson in an ordinary conversational voice. Pickup would have whispered.

'I thought I heard someone outside.' He listened for a moment, shrugged, and closed the door again.

'Who's in?' asked Linné.

'Only cook. Henry was going to take Jilly's

trunks to the station.'

'And Jill herself?'

'Oh, dashing about everywhere at once, as usual.'

Pickup wished that Jill could have been in on the scheme. She very nearly had been. That day at the bathing place he and Nick had speculated openly about the camp, but the damnfool idea hadn't at that time arisen. It had been hatched in the Augustiner beer cellar with Helmuth, actually starting with something Pickup had said, though nobody remembered that now. Jill had been voted out of the conspiracy mainly at Nicholson's urging. Though he always treated her with a kind of formal gallantry he was against the participation of girls in any thing he considered male or military. He produced some argument to the effect that it wouldn't be fair on her. Besides she was always hobnobbing with young Nazis, including S.S. cadets from Riem, and despite all her flippant jokes about the hierarchy – who had they met who didn't tell them?– seemed to find the uniforms and the swagger glamorous. Nick had said hotly that Christ, Helmuth was hardly a fanatical party man, which was true though he, too, had a curious double attitude–

Which reminded him. He said to Linné, 'Did you ask him about what's-his-name? Would he know which hut he's in?'

Linné said, 'No, we haven't. Thanks,' and to Nick, 'What was the name again?'

'Ihde. Klaus Ihde.'

Linné turned to the man with the question. He stared back for a moment, then spread his hands and muttered something. You didn't need German to know what he was saying. Pickup had an impulse to blurt out something that had been worrying him, off and on, ever since Christian Soldiers.

'Does it *have* to be this Klaus whatever his name is? I mean, there must be lots of equally deserving cases, perhaps more deserving...'

They stared at him. Only Linné looked as if he were speculating on the proposal. Nicholson said, 'Really, Mickup, if you want to chuck the thing we started with you might as well chuck the whole show.'

'Why only him, then? Why not lots of people?'

The speculation vanished from Linné's eyes. 'If you want them all back inside again, and us with them.' He glanced around to see if there was anything more from anyone and then began to shepherd the gaunt man through the door–

'Hallo,' said Jill. 'That's where you've all been, is it?' She was unbuttoning her coat as if she'd just come in and down the stairs. She looked questioningly at the man.

Nick said quickly, 'This is one of Aunt May's refugees from Germany.' He added, 'He was in that camp – we wondered if he might have news of Helmuth's old teacher, you know–'

'And did he?' She looked at the man almost with hostility.

'No. Didn't know the name. Said they're all numbers there, anyway.'

As they began to move again she snapped, 'Aren't you going to introduce me, then?'

Nick said. 'This is my sister. Um, this is ... um...'

'You don't know his name! Where *have* all your manners gone?' She thrust out her hand, wrist straight, fingers drooping, in a way that was at once boyish and imperious.

'It's Ehrlich,' said Linné.

The man bowed stiffly and briefly clasped her hand.

'Good afternoon, then, Herr Ehrlich,' and still in this cool, hostessy role Pickup had never seen her adopt before, 'Would you care for some tea?' When he blinked, she repeated the question in German. Nick frowned. Ian Nicholson said, 'We stopped at an A.B.C.'

'He might still be thirsty.'

But Ehrlich shook his head and smiled, the first time Pickup had seen him smile, and crammed his hat on his bristly head.

'Just a minute, then.' Pickup heard her dart into the kitchen, the protesting voice of the cook, Jill's clipped reply. She reappeared with a blue grocer's bag of sugar, another of coffee, half a thick Polony sausage, a bunch of grapes and an opened half bottle of brandy and, poo-pooing all protests, heaped them in his hands.

That night they beat around the pubs, but Jill came, and a girlfriend of Nick's who wasn't in the secret, either, of course, so it was rather a nice relief from the day's work. Nick and Pickup and the two girls finished up in a night-club with a bottle of gin delivered from the off-licence across the street and in the car going home Pickup held Jill's hand and fumbled with her knee. But later in bed the room started to tilt and wouldn't keep down and leaving it too late to get out he deposited a little puddle of sick in the middle of the faded carpet: and after mopping it up as best he could with hankies dipped in water from the jug and lying down again the sound of the name, like an old man clearing his throat of phlegm, thumped and echoed in his head.

## CHAPTER 3

*The gaunt man called Ehrlich sat in his room. He had cleared the crockery from the wash-stand; in its place was a pad of cheap lined paper. He adjusted his glasses and bowing his head close to the task began to write.*

My father's parents, *he began*, were both from Schongau in Bavaria. My mother's father was Austrian, from Linz. I was born in Schongau in May 1886 and thus am now fifty-two-years of age. After attending technical school I found employment with a firm of carriage-builders in Munich. During the 1914–18 war I enlisted in the infantry, being transferred later to the Motor Corps. I served on the Westfront and was wounded, On demobilisation I resumed my former employment but in 1922 joined the Bavarian Motor Works, with which concern I remained for ten years, when I set up my own small workshop to make a light motor cycle sidecar. This was in Weilheim, not far from my birthplace of Schongau. The enterprise slowly began to prosper and by 1935 I was employing eight craftsmen. In that year, however, several matters came to a head. There was increasing interference from the National Socialist authorities and the many bureaux they had set up to control business and the allocation of raw materials, and I was disinclined to undertake the flattery of petty officials, etc., necessary to maintain supplies. I inherited a modest property in Austria from my mother's family. Finally my beloved wife died of a breast cancer. As our daughter, the only child, was now happily married with two sweet children, I had no pressing reason to remain in a Germany whose government disturbed me and I resolved to retire to Austria. This was not easy for the movement of capital from the Reich was forbidden. I had to leave much behind. But in Austria I was able to make another start and once more, by the summer of 1937, I was employing three workers in a small enterprise. I learned with distress that my former small factory in Weilheim was not prospering under the new proprietor, to whom I had virtually given it, and that some of my craftsmen faced direction to munitions work in Stuttgart or Munich. I decided to go to Weilheim and offer the men employment in Linz if they could contrive to leave the Reich, which was increasingly difficult. At the frontier I was arrested and taken to police headquarters in Munich, where I learned that the story of hardship in Weilheim was untrue; it had been a ruse to attract me back across the frontier. My 'crime' was that of emigration.

The civil police were on the whole properly-behaved and fair, but interrogation by the secret state police, the so-called 'Gestapo', was conducted in a threatening and abusive manner. I was called a traitor and one who had robbed Germany of the technical knowledge and wealth that Germany had given me. I replied truthfully that I had forfeited nearly all my resources and had started up in Austria with the proceeds of the modest property there inherited from my mother; as for technical knowledge, I was unaware that motor-cycle sidecar designs represented any great mystery. At this the Gestapo officer became very angry and said that in Dachau I would have ample opportunity to regret my attitude.

So Dachau it was to be! Like everyone I had heard rumours of the concentration camp set up by the National Socialists in the very first year of their coming to power, 1933, but no one knew for sure what went on there. Reference in the German Press had been guarded, speaking mainly of the 're-education' of gypsies and work-shy elements who emerged from a spell in the camp fit and cleansed to work for National Socialism. In the Austrian papers there were different stories; it was said that some Communists and trade unionists had been retained in Dachau without trial for nearly four years, while many others had died there; that churchmen, teachers and many Jews – especially Jews accused of 'race-defilation', i.e. marrying Aryan girls – were confined along with hardened criminals and sexual perverts. My cell-mate, a fat man of about thirty, arrested because he had left a job in munitions production to run a fun-fair stall, sobbed all night. What would befall his wife and children? – though I remember thinking he was more truly distressed by his own separation from them. A widower, I was able to exercise the detachment that in the months to come would enable me to survive but which now, when I have survived, threatens to desert me.

*Ehrlich ceased writing and pondered. He scratched out the last sentence before resuming.*

On the third day following my arrest, June 16th, 1937, four of us were brought out of our cells and ordered into a closed van in the garage under the police headquarters. Already we were in the charge of the S.S., in the person of an armed N.C.O. of not more than nineteen years of age who spat in the face of one of the party, an elderly Jew, and in a harsh voice told us to sit 'to attention'. As the van left the police building in the Ettstrasse the clocks were chiming eleven. I imagined the visitors to the city gathered outside the Rathaus, only a short distance away, to watch the morning *Schaffertanz* of the carillon and the thought crossed my mind that if only I could spring from the van among them I would be safe, for would even the Nazis dare to shoot down a respectable middle-aged citizen before such an international assembly? Alas, studying the expression on the young S.S. man's face I knew he would not hesitate, As if reading my thoughts at this moment he shouted, 'Face the front, pig' and jabbed me in the chest with the heavy butt of his rifle. The blow made me exclaim aloud and he hit me again, lower in the abdomen, so that I had difficulty in breathing. Later he became more cheerful and smoking a small cigar told us that it wasn't so bad at Dachau – and that with any luck we would be dead before Christmas.

After a drive of rather less than half an hour the van stopped and started again several times. We heard shouted challenges and answers. Finally the door of the van was flung open and all at once three or four different voices were shouting at us to descend. Our 'initiation' to Dachau followed. First we stood rigidly to attention on a large expanse of square, facing the gatehouse, or 'Jourhaus' as we learned to call it. A more senior S.S. officer emerged from the Jourhaus and inspected us. The elderly Jew was wearing his medal ribbons and wound badge from 1914–18, as I might have done had I been arrested in my own home. This incensed the officer. He screamed. 'Where did you steal these ribbons, Jew?' and ripped them from the man's jacket. He added, 'The next Jew who masquerades as a loyal German will be made an example of.'

After the officer had conferred with a subordinate, calling out our names in turn to identify us, we were made to run to a hut where we were photographed, our heads shaved in the so-called barber's shop and our clothing and belongings taken away. Every item was meticulously noted. There was even a small buff envelope for each of us in which to put our rings, keys, etc. We were allowed to keep only a few handkerchiefs, our spectacles and R.M. 15 in money, and after some argument with the guards, the Jew his truss. Naked, we stood outside another hut for more than an hour, waiting until an S.S. doctor should deign to give us a perfunctory medical inspection. For us, luckily, it was summer and the weather warm. Later I was to see large groups of naked men waiting in icy winds or heavy frost. Next we were run to an old building, I believe once a munitions factory, that was being demolished but where there were still some primitive shower baths. The water was first scalding hot, then very cold, and in-vigorating. I began to feel hungry and thirsty but it was to be evening before we were allowed either food or drink. From the showers we doubled to a store-room where we were issued with prison uniforms. It was a customary joke, I learned later, for the orderlies to pick as ill-fitting uniforms as possible – short ones for long people, enormous sizes for very small men and so on. In our case the joke was played only on the fun-fair operator. He was fat with an unnatural fatness, possibly due to some deficiency. He was forced to squeeze into tight trousers against which his buttocks pressed tightly. The S.S. guards made loud jokes and throwing his boots or other clothing to the floor ordered him to pick them up again. When he bent over they pressed themselves obscenely against him. I was dismayed to notice that the orderlies, who themselves were prisoners, joined in the laughter.

I received 2 shirts, jacket and trousers in striped grey-green cloth, a cap of the same material, socks, boots, a toothbrush. The Jew's uniform was of blue and white stripes in a thinner cotton material. We were also given coloured tabs and numbers to be sewn to the left chest of the jacket and the right trouser leg. As an 'emigrant' mine was a blue triangle; the fun-fair comrade's was brown, the Jew's a black triangle, inverted, upon a yellow one to form a Star of David,

*Ehrlich paused here and counted the number of words he had written. It was 1500. He closed the pad and rubbed his eyes.*

Pickup pushed his way into the Baron of

Beef and quickly scanned the crowd of drinkers. No Nick, no Nicholson, no Linné. A man he knew from the engineering labs waved. Pickup mouthed 'Looking for someone' and backed out again. In the street he stood irresolutely for the moment. All the haunts tried and no sign of them. He'd meant to work – it was Thursday, with all Friday and Saturday to look forward to – but trying to settle to some structures after dinner had experienced a sudden panic of loneliness. The lodgings you had to have in your second year didn't help; his were down Lensfield Road, remote from the buzz of the town and cold and filled with dullards into the bargain. In college there had at least been Christopher Bright across the landing, and the thin dry music of his oboe – he played the oboe! – filtering under the door; when there was a violin as well that meant his girl-friend Sarah Friedlander was with him, who was Jewish and Girton and wore sandals but was quite sexy really, and none too careful with her skirts, and Pickup had usually thought of some excuse to go across about ten o'clock and be invited to stay for coffee or the drinking chocolate she sometimes brewed.

But Christ, he had been out of things that

first term a year before. The damp raw smell of the Cambridge autumn brought the sensation acutely alive again. Everyone said Cambridge was going to be so marvellous. He'd had visions of how it would be. Then somehow the weeks had gone by and he still had no friends. The hearties he hated, the aesthetes would look down on an engineer and anyway he secretly despised their affected voices and manners, his fellow engineers were dull, the two or three people from the same school were people he couldn't stand. Chris and Sarah were all right, but came from a world of chamber music and Fabians and co-ed schools that was unknown territory to him.

It was through Chris and Sarah that at last he'd met Nick and Co. They belonged to no recognisable camp. They were neither hearty nor aesthetic, neither rich-bug nor grubby scholarship. Only Nicholson was also an engineer. Nick was supposed to be reading Modern Languages and Linné Natural Sciences – though he was as often to be seen hobnobbing with the demonstrators in the engineering labs. Nick belonged to the Footlights and had done a rather funny turn in the summer term show, Nicholson to the O.T.C. and Linné to God knows how many strange societies. They got up to stunts and took risks but never familiar stunts or familiar risks: no night-climbing of the spire and pinnacles of Cambridge because Nick found it boring and Nicholson despised such purposeless hazard; no taking baths in women's colleges, it had been done too often before; but strange exploits that were sometimes gratifyingly talked about in the coffee-shops, like the night they'd spent in the ruins of haunted Borley Rectory, under the tall noiseless trees, drinking hot coffee laced with spirits and Pickup had dozed off and missed the moving radiance the others claimed to have seen... Pickup had decided instantly they were enviable and desirable and different. He had had the sense to exploit his flat northern accent and his grammar school instead of trying to conceal them. He told stories about the one in the other, developing a range of comical characters further and further removed from the drab facts with every telling but who became so real to the others that they began to invoke them in their own fancies. At the same time he watched his manners, at table or with servants, trying to pick up the public school graces which mattered.

He modelled his dress discreetly on theirs: when he appeared in his black prefect's blazer from school, with the college crest substituted for the school badge, Nicholson murmured, 'What a nice black coat, Mickup, but why spoil it with that badge?' – and back in his room that night he unpicked the crest with a razor blade. He ceased to wind around his neck the scratchy purple and white striped college scarf he had bought so eagerly from Ryder and Amies.

Now, a year later, he could own up to himself that he didn't always enjoy their company, Nicholson's least of all. In Nicholson's expression he could see, too often, disdain, even scorn. Even Nick's permanent high spirits sometimes seemed subtly to exclude him, like his sister's moods – when the two of them were together it could be beastly. And yet, at other times ... to lose them would be unbearable– Had he been too unenthusiastic about the German stunt? Well, no one had mentioned it much lately. He'd hoped it was forgotten. Hitching his gown back on to his shoulders, plunging his hands into his pockets, he turned morosely down Trinity Street.

The day in Dachau begins at 4.30 in winter,

3.30 in summer, when the siren outside Barrack Number 10 signals reveille. At once there is great activity. The food-orderlies must be ready for the command to run to the kitchens for the large canisters of thin brown fluid which is called 'coffee' and, every third morning, the kilo of bread which is each prisoner's ration. It is excellent bread. Others jostle to use the wash-fountains and lavatories, for although new barracks are always being added there was overcrowding all the time I was in Dachau. To use the lavatories is very important, because prisoners are not allowed back in the barracks during the day, there are no other latrines provided, nor may one rely on permission to relieve oneself being given by the guards. The prisoner who sits too long will be reviled by others waiting to take his place.

Then each bunk must be made up according to a precise rule: the straw palliasse squared off, the coverlet so arranged that its pattern of light blue and dark blue squares runs straight along the edges. Each locker must bear on its upper shelf the prisoner's spare shirt, folded to cover the full width of the shelf and presenting an angular surface 4 cm. high; on the lower shelf, the prisoner's utensils and bread ration; on the rack, his jacket and cap; at the bottom, his boots. The block-senior inspects each place and will not hesitate to demolish anything he says is not correct, shouting that he will not be punished for the laziness of some bourgeois or Jewish sh-t. This coarse word, for which I apologise, is used continually in Dachau by guards and prisoners alike, as noun, as adjective, as verb and in compound words. It occurs sometimes five or six times in one sentence. The reader may add it, if he wills, to such instances of speech as I report. I shall not trouble to record it each time.

Morning roll-call is at 5.45, an hour earlier in summer. The prisoners run to the great square, and assemble in lines facing the Jourhaus. The square echoes as each block-leader, who is a sergeant calls the tally of his 'protective captives' to the lieutenant in charge of the roll-call. The numbers must be added together and compared with the list of those who are in solitary confinement or hospital, etc. and the officer be satisfied that no one is missing. On occasion this may be very drawn out, when some paperwork is faulty, for example, and some prisoner who has been transferred to the punishment block or perhaps has died, cannot be accounted for. At other times, especially at the evening roll-call, the parade may be deliberately kept waiting for an hour or more as a punishment or simply on the whim of the officer. Yet the prisoner must stand at attention the whole time, though it may be freezing or raining or the cold wind blowing from the distant Alps and many of them are old or infirm or sick. No underclothes were issued during my time. It is true that they could be purchased at the canteen but the Jews particularly, whose prison clothes were made of lighter material, suffered greatly during the winter of 1937–38. Later many prisoners learned to wrap sheets of newspapers round their bodies or better still, the thick brown paper from emptied cement sacks. Drawers of paper were also useful during the bouts of diarrhoea which afflicted everyone. Permission to fall out to answer the calls of nature was rarely given, despite the fact that some of the older prisoners suffered from bladder troubles. A prisoner who was unable to contain himself was punished by having to wear 'sandwich-boards' proclaiming the nature of his offence.

After morning roll-call the prisoners are marched away for work or for drill. For most of my imprisonment it was work because of the rebuilding of the camp and hard as this was it was preferable to the drilling which I experienced in the first weeks, when to fatigue and the ever-present risk of a blow or a kick was added the senselessness of unproductive effort. Some of the drills were impossibly arduous, such as having to do a slow 'knees-bend' to the count of ten and then spring to standing position, over and over again until many men fainted, at which the young guard would kick and abuse them. Others were quite sadistic. On one occasion we were divided into two lines facing each other, and each man made to punch his opposite number in the face until he drew blood. Other indignities I cannot bring myself to describe.

For work the prisoners are organised quite separately from their barrack disposition. That is to say, members of the same block do not normally belong to the same work party. Presumably this is to reduce the possibility of conspiracy among prisoners thrown together continuously. It does mean, however, that one meets, prisoners from other categories which does not happen in the barracks. Even the Jews, rigorously segregated in accommodation and dress, are distributed. One may find oneself working alongside a Jew, an Earnest Bible Student, a Communist or a Gypsy – all categories, in fact, except the hardened criminals who are in the camp for 're-education' and who, I observed, all enjoy privileged jobs such as block-orderlies, kitchen staff, store hands, etc.

Latterly I was employed on levelling a mound of rubble towards the northern end of the camp, the material being used to provide the foundations of further rows of huts to be erected beyond the twelve rows completed by the time I left Dachau. The rubble had to be loaded into wheelbarrows and transported at the double a distance of some two to three hundred metres, the guards all the time shouting to us to get a move on. Once a young prisoner, I forget of which category, tripped and fell. This was common enough but the guard, to amuse himself, made the young man complete the distance carrying the loaded barrow on his back. Another prisoner, working in the next gang to mine, was unfortunate enough to drop a pick into the deep drainage canal. Although it was still March the guards ordered him to dive into the water and recover it. When after several attempts he did so, they threw it back and made him dive again. Eventually he dived and did not come up. The guards laughed and jeered but made anxious perhaps by the looks of the other prisoners, or the proximity of the S.S. Barracks beyond the canal and the possibility of being seen by a commissioned officer, then endeavoured to rescue the poor youth. It was too late. The guards are ignorant and unskilled youths who but for the National Socialist regime would have been fitted only for the basest employment, if any at all. In general they display an envious hatred for any prisoner from the intellectual or professional classes. Spectacles they regard as a sure indication, and anyone wearing them is called an 'eye-glass snake'. When my own glasses were knocked from my face by a guard soon after my arrival at Dachau and stamped upon and smashed, it was almost a relief, though without glasses I cannot see to read the largest print and the camp library, composed of books 'donated' by the prisoners themselves, is one of the few reminders of civilisation beyond those dread walls.

What I found, if anything, more dismaying was that the same attitude is shared by many of the prisoners. Those from meaner walks of life, especially the habitual criminals, not only maintain that in Dachau everyone is equal, which is true, but that they are just as good in every way as the former surgeon or engineer or pastor, which is not necessarily the case. Some of them go further and ape the behaviour and attitudes of the guards. The S.S. men pride themselves on their toughness, so the prisoners will demonstrate that they are even tougher. They box together as the S.S. box together. They march and drill as if they were soldiers of a crack regiment. They improvise belts and pad their caps to imitate the S.S. uniform. Far from resenting the regime which has condemned them to barbaric imprisonment they become its patriotic admirers, threatening violence to anyone who criticises it in their hearing and discussing with enthusiasm such exploits as the enforced union with Austria which took place during my captivity.

I have digressed from the daily routine of the camp which I set out to describe. Work pauses at twelve, signalled by the siren. Dinner is a stew of beans or cabbage and potato. On a good day there may be a little tripe or other offal. Then work again from one o'clock until evening roll-call at 6.30. Supper is ground rice in skim milk or perhaps some cheese or a salt herring. By the time it has been fetched and eaten only a little time, half an hour at the most, remains before the siren signals to make ready for bed. The beds, in fact are wooden bunks built in great structures like honeycombs, thirty-six or fifty-four men to each, three tiers high. When the intake of new prisoners outstrips the building of new barracks, as happened particularly during the early summer of this year, when large numbers of Jews from Austria were brought in, not every man can enjoy even this rough comfort, and many must sleep on the bare floor. Twenty minutes after the first siren it sounds again for 'lights out'. Another day at Dachau has ended.

If you half-closed your eyes and concentrated on the approaching car, especially if it was Nuvolari's Auto-Union, it seemed to be coming in an unwavering line, like a bullet, aloof to meanderings of the road ... which in fact was the case, Pickup realised: on this long, sinuous stretch the art would be not to follow every curve in the road but aim at the famous straight line which is the shortest distance – yet Nuvolari's arms, brown and bare and hairy below the short sleeves of his yellow pullover, were working prodigiously as the car was upon them, then past, blunt bullet-nose, flat silvery-white paint, long trailing tail, high bursts of engine noise as Tazio went down through the gears, not quite as high and exciting as the Merc.'s but still pretty marvellous. It was Pickup's favourite vantage point. The trouble was that Nicholson would be agitating again in a minute to move nearer the Finish, where they wouldn't see anything–

'Come on,' said Nicholson. 'We want to see the finish. There's only three laps to go.'

'Let's just watch von Brauchitsch through.'

The Donington Grand Prix, postponed from its original date in September because of the Crisis: Nicholson had been going to bring Nick Amering but Nick had got a cold and had cried off a hundred miles each way in an open Morgan and Linné was going off on some mysterious errand of his own. Pickup had finally gone round to Nick's rooms in Trinity, not expecting to find anyone there, and Nick, dressing gowned, drinking whisky with Nicholson, had said carelessly, typically, 'Take Michael instead', and Nicholson had been obliged to ask him, though he hadn't looked overjoyed about it. Actually it hadn't proved a bad day at all: an exhilarating run over from Cambridge in the Morgan, wedged next to Nicholson in the little cylindrical fuselage, admiring his trickery with the hand-throttle and straight-pull gear-lever, peering ahead between the wide-set front wheel and the massive obtruding cylinder of the vee-twin Villiers. Nicholson had been friendly if dominant, and though Pickup couldn't be sure whether it was good or bad under the circumstances, hadn't alluded once to the stunt–

'Here he comes.' Brauchitsch was driving with one hand in bandages, lying only fourth or fifth, but he took the sinuous stretch more excitingly than anyone: no straight line for him but a series of violent tangents to the curves, the long nose of the Mercedes wagging, the engine note like trumpets. Howling into the corner he arrogantly swept past an out-classed English E.R.A.

'Picture of a first-class power showing up a second,' said Nicholson. 'What machinery, what organisation! God, we've a long way to catch up.'

They pushed through the crowds, the stupid crowds they'd become after a day in Nicholson's company: gaping ignorantly, making ignorant remarks, preferring to throng the refreshment marquees and drink pints of beer from waxed-paper cups – in the middle of an October afternoon – rather than watch the race. The closer to the grandstand and pit area the denser, in both senses, they got. The nearest spot to the Finish Nicholson could find was about three hundred yards back down the straight but they saw Nuvolari take the flag, then Lang, Seaman and the others. Almost the greatest applause was for the bandaged-hand von Brauchitsch. Perhaps it was the stupid crowd who knew nothing about motor-racing displaying traditional British sportsmanship, et cetera, for anyone competing against a handicap, especially if he were at all a flamboyant character, as Manfred von B. certainly was. But odd that these ordinary yobs should be so friendly towards the Germans with whom they had so nearly been at war – would be yet, according to Philipp Linné. Odder still that they should adopt as their hero the most Germanic of the Germans, nephew of a general, while according to Seaman, the Englishman who drove for Mercedes, had finished third and was a Cambridge man, incidentally, only a dutiful enthusiasm.

He heard pompous music funnelling from

the blurry public address: it would be the Italian national anthem, for Nuvolari. Above the grandstand the Italian, British and German flags fluttered from a trio of flag-poles. The music changed to the stirring wa-wa-wa of *Deutschland Uber Alles* for Lang. Pickup started to say 'Come on, let's–' but stopped. Nicholson remained erect and motionless, oblivious of the crowd starting to move around him, the little muscles of his cheek tight, like springs.

Reading over what I have already set down I am aware that I have not made Dachau the monstrous place I know it to be. The descriptions of petty routine and arduous labour are not so different from the accounts of field punishment centres and military prisons I remember hearing during my service in 1914–18. But when I try to describe even those incidents of gross brutality which I myself witnessed my pen is unequal to the challenge. What reasonable citizen of this country can be expected to believe stories of men flogged with leather whips, precisely 25 strokes, neither more nor less; of men cruelly strung to trees and left all day; of a punishment cellar adminis-tered by a misshapen pervert and murderer so evil that even the guards shun him. Besides, it is true that a proportion of the 'protective captives' do linger in Dachau in comparative immunity. After one year any prisoner's chances of survival must automatically be reckoned to have improved; by now he has learned the first rule of life in the camp, which is never to be noticed. The man who stands out from the rest, whether by his behaviour or by some physical peculiarity which he cannot help, is the man who must fear the most attention from the guards. With luck the old Dachauer, as he begins to call himself, may even have won a favoured job.

Let me rather try to describe the less violent but no less evil effects of the place upon my fellow-men. So fearful is the first impression, so threatening the 'initiation' – often as a jest the guards will march new prisoners to a remote corner of the camp and order them to dig their own graves – that many newcomers straightway lose any will to live. Suicide is not difficult in Dachau. One can throw oneself at the electrified fence, or be shot down from the machine-gun towers before reaching it. The guards will often, half-mockingly, half-intentionally, provide a length of rope with crude directions how to use it. But beware: an unsuccessful attempt will cost the luckless bungler twenty-five lashes.

Some who do not have the courage to attempt suicide sink into a state of lethargic despair. Known as 'Mohammedans', for what reason I am not clear, they exist as if in a trance. I must add that it is my own class, the middle-class, especially those members of it without strong political or religious convictions, which is most commonly afflicted in this way. A small shopkeeper, say, abruptly deprived of the modest position lent him by his business, stripped of the authority as head of the family which in Germany still counts for much, has nothing left to buoy him up. In general it is the political prisoners, particularly the Communists who have now been in Dachau for five years, who preserve the highest morale. Next to them come the Earnest Bible Students, or God's Witnesses as I believe they are known in England. Their offence is failing to acknowledge Adolf Hitler as supreme authority, though the younger ones are also persecuted because they refuse military service. Any student is free to be released if only he will sign an abdication of his views and, in the case of a younger man, agree to military service. Every student is encouraged to do so soon after arrival at the camp with twenty-five lashes. Yet the vast majority remain steadfast. My experience of these men was that they were narrow-minded, dogmatic, trying always to persuade others to their faith, yet excellent comrades who would always help anyone they could. The guards, for their part, treated them with a vindictiveness second only to that they reserved for the Jews, yet at the same time frequently chose them, because of their industry and dependability, as their personal servants.

My own survival I attribute to several circumstances. As I have related, the loss of my dear wife and my own decision to uproot myself from my homeland had given me a certain detachment, even stoicism. Of course, I bitterly reviled myself for re-entering Germany and exposing myself to arrest, but even this anguish was reduced when on March 11th–12th, 1938, the 'Union' with Austria was imposed and I was able to reflect that fate would have overtaken me whatever I had done. Indeed it is likely that my release from Dachau after ten months was directly due to the need to accommodate the large numbers of Austrians, especially Jews, who were now being transported thither. Whole trains would arrive in the morning within the S.S. barracks just outside the camp.

I had always enjoyed good health, which in Dachau was of great importance, for to report sickness could be dangerous and treatment, if obtainable at all, was perfunctory. Perhaps nothing was more distressing to me than to have to watch the suffering and decline of those who suffered chronic ailments or had the handicap of hernias, etc. Equally important, I had never believed that as engineer I was a mere technician. I had always taken some interest in the arts and sciences and was an amateur student and collector of what are sometimes called 'bygones' – the implements and tools and indeed mechanical devices of our forefathers. On occasion I had contributed articles and photographs to learned journals, and though I had to leave the bulk of my collection in Weilheim, in the museum there, I was able to take my notes with me to Austria.

It may be imagined with what pleasure I discovered, after some weeks, a new arrival who shared my interest in the bygones of Bavaria, and with whom I was able to discuss the subject during precious periods of recreation. We formed a friendship of the kind which constitutes the noblest of Dachau's few compensations. Such friends sustain and protect each other, share whatever meagre comforts they can buy from the canteen or may be allowed to receive in parcels, even share each other's punishment. Yet my friend and I came from quite different walks of life, I an engineer and small businessman, he a professor of the university. I will refer to him only as K., for he was not released when I was set free and may still be within those dread walls.

By strange chance – or was it design? – some young men, students, sought me out only a short time after I arrived in England, having heard of me through the organisaion which assisted my admission to this country. After asking many general questions about the layout and administration of the camp one of them suddenly asked if I knew K. I was astonished but the secretive habit which every Dachauer learns stood me in good stead. Instinctively I denied any knowledge of my friend. I knew nothing of the young men except that they had an acquaintance with the refugee organisation, and one of them was undoubtedly a German though I could not place his accent precisely. I have often wondered since if I thus impeded some intercession that might have been made on K.'s behalf, but the risk of betrayal seemed greater than the possibility of help.

K.'s offence was in a classical and honourable tradition. His classes at the university had been extremely popular, for his method had been that of the Greek philosopher Socrates, teaching his pupils by questioning them. He taught them to test all that was told them against logic and common sense and humanity. Inevitably this brought him into conflict with the principles of National Socialism. After several warnings he was wakened in his rooms at four o'clock one morning and taken away. He admitted ruefully that his own vanity in persisting with his classes for the pleasure of the attention they brought him was partly his undoing. He told me that the authorities had sought to blacken his name and dispel any lingering respect among the students by accusing him also of immoral practices. A young male student was bribed or intimidated into making a disgusting charge against him.

Nothing could have been more foreign to this wise and sensitive man. He taught me to avoid the depths of despair with the aid of intellectual effort, not only by 'escapist' means, such as our discussions of our hobby, but also by studying our plight in an analytical way to see if one might strengthen one's endurance. In the absence of strong political or religious convictions or family ties – K. was unmarried – what could we hold on to? (Not that family ties always sustained; it could happen that a prisoner pined so grievously for his wife or children that he sunk into an abyss of despair. Those that did adjust themselves found that after a few months they could no longer remember the appearance of their beloved ones.) K. suggested the resolve should be to defeat the object of the concentration camp, which he had decided was to destroy the personality – we had evidence of its success all around us. It was not enough simply to survive. One had to survive as oneself. If we could emerge at the end with our identities intact, however straitened our bodies, the victory would be ours. Meanwhile each day endured was a battle won.

We did not often discuss the possibility of escape, for in truth there seemed none and neither of us was physically equipped for any desperate feat, but the moral problem interested K. In the very few instances of escape from Dachau preserved in the camp lore the S.S. had taken reprisals against the remainder of the prisoners and in particular against the barrack block to which the fugitive had belonged. Was a prisoner therefore justified in trying to escape should the opportunity offer itself? K. insisted that he was, because to do so was the ultimate assertion of the personality. It would be more than a private victory over the system. It would be a resounding public one.

Only when I came to be released, as I shall presently relate, did this brave human being falter: even then he recovered and at my insistence promised that he would maintain his resolve to survive, and survive as himself. Lately I have begun to suffer frequent nightmares when the cruelty of Dachau seems to press upon me anew and the world of my little room, indeed of the teeming, innocent city outside, becomes insubstantial. At such times my only comfort is to conjure up some recollection of the moments of tranquillity which, strange as it may seem, the prisoner in Dachau may experience. Those morning roll-calls which could be so cold and dark and cruel could also, in spring and early summer, reveal such beauty as I had never dreamed of: skies high and clear and subtle in colouring as day dawned, with streamers of cloud tinted all the colours of the rainbow and edged with gold, while to the south-east the sun would light up the distant white peaks of the Alps. Or in the evening, a west wind would sometimes bring the sound of children's voices from the married quarters of the S.S. barracks. I saw men weep to hear it. I remember Christmas when the S.S. with the sentiment that even the most degraded of my countrymen retain, set up a Christmas tree. I remember a concert given within the camp by some of the Jewish musicians and entertainers who came in after the Union. But mostly I remember the precious hour every Sunday afternoon when that Socrates and his last, least clever disciple could stroll between the young poplars of the camp avenue and eagerly discuss the roasting spits of old Munich.

Linné came in carrying a cardboard box, not very big but heavy enough to *clunk* solidly on to the table next to the model of the camp. 'A present for me?' said Nick. 'How kind.' He was better again but the meeting had been called in his room anyway.

Linné said, 'The answer. Simple. Infallible. Just what we've been needing all along.'

Pickup felt another tiny shiver inside him.

Linné was so matter-of-fact, he *meant* it. The box was thick brown cardboard, stapled at the corners, identified only by a narrow yellow label along the bottom of one side. Linné took off the lid, and lifted out something wrapped in brown waxed paper. You could smell the solid factory smell. Linné unfolded the wrapping. It was dark green, with a dial, a milled brass knob in the centre, terminals, a massive back plate drilled at each corner. Pickup guessed what it was at once. He said, 'The Infernal Machine?'

Linné laughed. 'A good name for it. I took a little trip to the Beaton works in Rugby. I knew they'd have one there.' He examined the specification plate, wiping it clean of grease with his finger. 'We enter the camp as dutiful BBL electricians, go to the turbine house, connect this little toy into circuit, set it for the pre-arranged hour and leave again. By the time it is due to function we can be miles away – we might even be out of the Reich altogether.' He paused in admiration of the advantages of the device.

Nicholson was nodding his head in endorsement. It was Nick who asked the obvious, 'And it deals with – what? The electrified wire?'

'The searchlights, too, if we choose our circuit properly. Our friend inside has been warned of the time. He is ready and waiting. His best place is obviously here' – he indicated it on the model. 'The – let me see – north-east corner. It is least well covered by the machine gun towers, really only by the one here in the middle of the north side. In the confusion and sudden darkness, over the wall he goes and away.' He trotted two fingers of his right hand across the model and into the air, over the moat and fence and wall, to alight again outside–

Nicholson said, 'Barbed wire is still barbed wire, even if the current is cut. And I thought Mickup said the outer wall was something like twenty feet high.' The elation that had been bubbling up in Pickup, because suddenly it all seemed so simple and safe, subsided again.

Linné looked displeased but not downcast. 'Helmuth can surely think of something. A rope ladder, perhaps. Our contribution will take care of the most difficult obstacle. With that neutralised the battle is surely half won. More than half.'

'The other thing,' said Nicholson, 'is do we know that it will necessarily be a dark night? Supposing there is a full moon.'

Linné pouted. 'We can look in the almanac. Besides in November, as it will be, we can almost count on fog and cloud.'

Pickup was emboldened to raise a point. 'And Helmuth *can* get the message to the man inside – the day and the time and everything?'

Nick said casually, 'So he says.' He seemed even less concerned about this part of the stunt than about the rest of it. No one else pursued the matter. Linné began to wrap up the device again.

Nicholson straightened his back, as if he'd weighed up the pros and cons and made a decision. He said, 'It sounds on to me. When do we go?'

Nick said, 'Jill's birthday is the seventh.'

Nicholson had his diary out. 'That's a Monday. She'd have the party that night?'

'I suppose so.'

'We might as well go for the weekend. It's a long way. I suggest we take the night boat from Harwich on the Friday. We'd be in Munich – when?'

'Saturday night,' said Linné.

'Hooray,' said Nick. 'We can do the beer-cellars.'

Pickup said. 'When would we be back?'

They looked at him. Nick said, 'Oh, about

the Wednesday. Why?'

'I – I hadn't reckoned on missing so many lectures and so on. Besides, what about the college...?'

'What?– Oh, we all get exeats for the weekend, then send a telegram to say we got held up or the car broke down or something.'

'We're not going by car, are we?'

'Who's to know?'

Nicholson said coldly, 'Look, if you're not keen, Mickup, you don't have to come. We could manage with three, couldn't we?' He glanced at Nick, then Linné.

'Of course I'm keen. It's just that...' He tried to think what to say. Half of him wanted to get out while the opportunity was there, the other half wanted desperately to say yes–

Linné said, 'With three? If necessary. We can perhaps call on this Helmuth–'

'That's all right, then,' said Nicholson.

Pickup felt the bottom slipping out of his world. He *did* want to go, they couldn't leave him behind but already it was too late – the way Nicholson had said, 'That's all right, then–'

Nick said suddenly, 'I say, it's not question of the – er, expense, is it? You know, we don't expect you to–'

Pickup grasped for the lifeline. Actually it had been rather worrying, though on the summer trip the others had tacitly subsidised him. 'Well, it is a bit difficult ... but I couldn't...'

'Oh, come on. Don't be so silly.'

Linné said, 'By the way, all the travel – I can get it through my father's office in London. It need not cost us a penny.'

'That's marvellous,' said Pickup. It really was so marvellous that for the moment it eclipsed every other consideration.

'Now let's go and have some beer,' said Nick.

It was as close as that.

## CHAPTER 4

Ploughlands, onion-topped churches, a lone factory chimney, a white lamp glowing in an otherwise darkened signal box, and always the blot shapes of woodland: the train hammered south through a blue dusk. Pickup, though stale and bored after twelve hours, was in no hurry for the journey to end. While they were still in the smoky, littered compartment they were – well, just tourists. He let his eyes adjust from the vague dark landscape beyond the window to the reflection in it, seeing almost with nostalgia the sleek steel knob for the heating, the framed brown photographs of Lindau, Ulm and the Tittisee, the pages of the *Continental Daily Mail* that Nick, now dozing, had managed to scatter everywhere. In the far corner the man in brown suit and big brown bow tie continued to pore over the pages of figures which had occupied him since he boarded at Frankfurt. The man who looked like a parody of a German, with shaven bullet head and wing collar under massive jowls, continued to sleep. Not until Nuremburg, curiously, had they had anyone in uniform, a boy in the short square jacket and breeches of the Luftwaffe who clattered aboard as the train began to pull out of the station hung with banners and braggart signs that this was the high city of National Socialism.

Nicholson had sought to involve him in conversation in halting mixtures of German and English to which the cadet responded shyly. He was seventeen, he hoped soon to start flying training. He had already flown fourteen hours in the Vampyr sailplane, he intended to be a fighter pilot flying the Me

109. Nicholson nodded approvingly. He himself would enter the army when he had finished university. Had the cadet perhaps come across his friend or, rather, bringing in Nick, his friend's friend Helmuth – what was the name again? – who was a famous glider and gave much time to teaching Hitler Youth boys? Wanting to join in, Pick-up had appealed to Linné, who had sulkily interpreted, but the German smiled shyly and withdrew into a book.

Pickup's eyes strayed again to the squat leather case, more like a bag only with a zip-fastener, a thing he'd never seen on luggage before, which Philipp Linné had stowed with careful nonchalance in the rack, At the customs – the Dutch customs, thank God – it had actually started to TICK, as in a Three Stooges film or something! Pickup had felt himself reddening, convinced everyone must be staring. But Nick had burst out laughing: real, helpless laughter. And of course it was very funny, as long as it didn't do it again going into das Reich.

God! That had been no laughing matter. Old Linné swaggered through coolly as you please. With his name and everything it might just have been all right if they'd rummaged... But honestly, it was like entering

Witchland in a fairy-story. In the summer it had been fine, bowling in by car in that Alpenland sunshine, finding it all romantic and exciting: in that bleak siding by flat fields on a raw morning he had felt iron gates clanging shut behind them. Oh, the frontier officials had been polite, wishing them an enjoyable stay ... but there was something terribly unnatural about it, compared with other frontiers. Suddenly he saw what it was: no bustle, no noise. No one talked, no one presumed to be in a hurry. They waited obediently. And why was that old lady who looked a bit like Aunty Carrie led off into a back room? *And why had she not rejoined the train?*

Saturday evening roll-call was often earlier and invariably shorter than on full working days, so that the guards off duty could ponce themselves up in their best uniforms with death's head insignia and go into Munich for drinking and women. Today the hoarse voices echoed and re-echoed as the sky darkened and the lights of the Jourhaus grew brighter and from the watch-towers the searchlights sprang on to shine along the drab grey walls and wire. Klaus Ihde rocked gently on the balls of his feet, a tip that Rolf

111

Ehrlich, an old soldier, had given him to ease standing at attention: just enough to take the weight off the heels for a moment, not enough to make the body move and thus violate the first rule of survival, which was never to attract attention. God, he schemed and jostled for a place in a centre rank, among other reliable survivors, as determinedly as once he might have schemed for the best table in the Café Luitpold after the theatre. Tonight perhaps he would take himself to the theatre, beginning with, say, shaving – stroke by stroke of the razor as it cut its swathes through the thick foam on his face, the companionable smell of the copper water heater in the steamy little bathroom of his apartment in the Viktoriaplatz; a glass of wine as he dressed ... but they were only words, words, words. Of what had wine tasted, how had hot water felt? The sensations had gone, the exercise of reliving this or the other sweet routines occupied a shorter and shorter time, the images he could summon were less and less substantial. With Rolf, to whom he had taught the trick, it had been easier: that craftsman's mind of his fastened on the details of objects. Oh God, the wind was already chill. Could he endure another

112

winter? Would release never come? After a spate in the summer there'd been hardly any lately. If only they'd bring some more Jews in, they might clear out some of the others. No, that was ignoble. The stern bourgeois moralist, old Ehrlich, would never have approved...

They were shouting out the numbers of the prisoners for punishment. He listened anxiously; there'd been a period when secure in his anonymity he'd been confident for months on end that his number would never be called. But now there were these curious messages that had been reaching him through the canteen orderly with the broken nose, an old time professional thief if ever he saw one ... what folly to have trusted him...

It was all right: the numbers had ceased. Six to resume punishment drill, one luckless soul for the tree, two for flogging. They ran forward to the brightly-lit area immediately in front of the Jourhaus, cuffed and kicked on the way by the guards. A couple of bible students; the routine twenty-five lashes if they wouldn't abdicate their stubborn, humourless beliefs. God, he would sign anything that was asked, renounce anything, here amongst these for whom he had no

113

regard. It had only been his conceit for the admiration of a few students that made him persist before *hubris,* as the Greeks knew it... Escape, the messages proposed. He had friends outside, it seemed. Escape! How could a man escape who was forty-one years old and after a year in Dachau weighed but forty-four kilograms?

Buildings, sidings, gantries became more plentiful along the line. They rattled more and more often across points. Nicholson, already neater and trimmer than any of them, stood up and fished in his case for a toilet bag and stepping past the air force boy with a soldierly smile went along the corridor for a wash. Nick Amering stretched and reached for the shoes he'd kicked off. Pickup, looking out again as they went through another station, saw its name with a sudden shock. He swivelled round, pointing, his mouth opening to say something to Nick but catching Linné's furiously mimed warning in time. Ten minutes later they were coming to rest in the brightness of the Hauptbanhof.

On the platform Linné said to Nicholson, 'For God's sake, when we came through you-know-where – you were in the lavabo –

guess what bloody Michael did! Started pointing and jumping about as if he'd seen a ghost. If I hadn't stopped him he would most likely have shouted out the name or something. And in front of that Luftwaffe kid!'

Nicholson said nothing but looked at Pickup with his face set at its coldest and most contemptuous, as if wondering if it wouldn't be better to jettison him straight-away. Pickup felt an impulse to lash out, quelled it, said lamely, 'I didn't realise we would come through there. Anyway, who got him interested in us?'

But Nick was already turning it into a joke. 'You should have said in a loud voice, "Isn't that where we were supposed to get off?"' In the beer-cellar restaurant of the Schottenhammel Hotel an hour later the incident was ready for polishing and fram-ing and ornamentation, along with Philipp Linné's ticking luggage, as preliminary pearls in the long string of pearls which Nick and he would make of the adventure. Washed and changed into the black blazer and smooth flannels, one super half-litre of beer already down, another ordered, Pickup felt warm and contented. For the moment the rag was only a rag again, for a moment even the nagging unease at being so far, so illicitly, from college–

'Do you remember what day it is?' said Nick suddenly.

They thought for a second. 'November the fifth,' said Pickup, who'd been aware all the time but didn't want to admit that he too hadn't forgotten.

'Nine o'clock,' said Nick. 'In Cambridge they'll be getting going nicely.'

'Beating round the pubs,' said Nicholson.

'Whooping round the bonfires,' said Pickup.

'Firing rockets down Petty Cury.'

'Knocking off policemen's helmets.'

'Kidding themselves,' said Nicholson quietly, 'that they're being so desperate. The fools.'

The waitress brought the beer, the four tall glasses cupped carelessly – but unspilling – in the palm of her hand. She was enormously fat, with deep pits of dimple in the elbows of her massive arms. As she waited with pad and pencil for their orders for food, patient, even motherly, Pickup sensed her tiredness and was filled, he didn't know why, with a welling love for her until he saw Nicholson wrinkling his nose at her faint stale smell and guiltily grinned. He looked around the restaurant: low-ceilinged, all pale woodwork and brown walls and dulled gold, filled but not crowded with solid Münch-eners, scarcely a uniform to be seen. It was impossible that ... but Linné was lifting his glass and murmuring a toast to the success of their venture. He drank.

Emil lay quite still, waiting for the shivering to return. The soreness at his back seemed to have thickness, to be a cushion of sore-ness, some centimetres thick, that came between him and the stiff, rustling mattress. For the thousandth time his tongue touched and explored the sharp point of the broken tooth and the swollen lips beyond. His mouth seemed full of salt, his nose of the strong smells of straw and raw pinewood and tobacco and sweat and men's bowels. He heard breathing, low muttering, once the scratching of a match, several times the rasp of gas expelled from the rectum. He tried to think of Jehovah, stern and bearded and robed and mighty, the ranks of people dividing before him as the waters before the bow of a great ship. When the shivering didn't return, he slept.

Sunday morning and church bells bonged

117

out over the city as Jill Amering came flying into the hotel lobby, a red and white tam o'shanter on her head, a wide tweed skirt swinging round those stalky, troubling legs. 'Hallo, where's Nick? *Michael,* how nice – Helmuth's outside with the car, and you're all to come to lunch – how about *that?*' Nick, emerging this moment from the little lift, she embraced and kissed. Pickup, still glowing from her greeting, felt only the slightest pang of jealousy.

Outside Helmuth posed behind the wheel of the vons and zus' old Horch, a make that had since been swallowed up by Auto-Union. He waved, slid athletically from the driving seat, said to Michael warmly, 'My dear fellow,' thumped Nick on the back, saluted Nicholson, shook hands with Linné, whom he hadn't met before. They all squeezed in. Turning down Prielmayer-strasse he said in his careful old-boy English, 'Too bad I didn't get to your country to see you all in the summer. That infernal crisis spoiled everything.' And whose fault was it, thought Pickup. He wasn't sure about Helmuth. To be so casual and civilian in this boot-stamping, flag-waving country, to be so concerned about some old university friend – that was obviously to be admired. Taking

118

the pictures had been hellish brave even if as an ace sports pilot he had rather special opportunities. Suppose he'd been caught, it didn't bear thinking about. At the same time some lingering puritan strain implanted at home and school and Christian Soldiers which even Cambridge hadn't been able to eradicate made Pickup disapproving of such a playboy existence, ski-ing all winter, sailing and gliding and dancing ... besides, how old was he? The brushed-back hair was glossy brown, the profile as he turned to speak to Jill at his side as sculpted as Ramon Navarro, the film star's. He'd let it be known that he did a bit of acting himself for the Munich film studios, or was it stunt-flying? Or both? But the hands on the wheel of the Horch could almost be his father's hands, who was forty or even forty-five. Did they feel Jill, did she sometimes – and the skin of his neck was, well, not actually wrinkled but somehow half a size too loose. There was a great deal of gold in his flashing smile. No, jealousy didn't come into it. Better Helmuth than those blond gods. Besides, in a way it was comforting to have Helmuth around, because then Nicholson or Linné wouldn't be tempted to move in, which would be unbearable. It was envy, perhaps, for his man-of-the-worldliness ... he had to admit it was damned flattering to be treated as an equal by Helmuth.

Helmuth said, 'First we go a little spin round the city, but not so far, because petrol is rationed since you were last here.'

Jill said, 'What he means is that we can't go to the house yet because the vons and zus expect us all to be in church by now. We went to St. Lukas in the Mariannenplatz, agreed?'

Helmuth seemed to have picked a route that led through ever more grandiose squares – from the Karls- to the Max- to the Odeonsplatz, marble columns succeeding marble columns, great blank white façades, endless colonnades, acres of concrete and the blood red banners hanging limply, this still hazy morning, from the ranks of flagpoles. Pickup struggled with his smattering of architectural lore to work out why he disliked it while being nevertheless impressed. He said to Nick loudly, hoping to be overheard by Jill, 'It's the scale that's all wrong. It crushes you – makes you feel small and tired instead of ... letting you rise to it.'

Linné frowned and mouthed at him.

'*Now* what's the matter?'

Linné said, 'In this country it's as well to

keep your opinions about National Socialist achievement to yourself, even at the expense of depriving the rest of us of them.'

Helmuth showed profile and the glint of gold teeth as he laughed. 'I do not think anyone is going to get locked up for saying he doesn't like the House of German Art.'

'I wouldn't be so sure,' said Linné.

Helmuth's smile vanished. He snapped out something in German. Linné replied with a shrug.

Nicholson said, 'What was that about?'

'Nothing.'

'Stop squabbling, the lot of you,' said Jill.

They parked the car and strolled first in the English Garden, then across the bridge in the narrow strip of park by the Isar, green and clean and swirling like the sea in the picture of the Icefoam tin.

'Here in the open one may talk freely, even in Germany,' said Helmuth. 'It cannot even matter if we quarrel, eh?' He linked his arm companionably in Pickup's, so that even in the open air Pickup got a good whiff of eau de Cologne.

'What was that tiff with Philipp?' Linné was ahead with Nicholson.

'Nothing, dear chap,' said Helmuth.

Nick said, 'He's so obsessed by how awful

der Reich is–'

'But he bit my head off for even criticising the architecture.'

'Exactly. That was to snub Helmuth. He forgets that Helmuth is a German, living in Germany.'

Jill said, 'He may not be a fanatic supporter of the Partei but that doesn't mean he wants to listen to a lot of stuff from someone who's just as German except that he happens to have a Swiss passport...'

'Is that it?'

Helmuth lightly squeezed Pickup's arm. 'We are all human, are we not?' He changed the subject. 'I hope no one expects too grand a lunch, On Sunday one must cook only an *Eintopfgericht,* a one-pot meal, you know' – his o-sounds were very pure and round and o-ish.

'Even the vons and the zus?' said Nick, laughing.

'Especially the vons and zus,' said Jill. 'You think they'd overlook any chance to save on feeding us?'

Pickup was smitten with the unbelievableness of it all. Only two days before he'd been in the engineering labs at Cambridge, loading a beam to breaking point in the Buckton machine. In Cambridge now they'd be filing, white-surpliced out of chapel. Yet he walked and talked by the Isar – the sheer awful distance between where he was and where he ought to be tugged at him. Tomorrow he was supposed to be at lectures but even if he ran and caught a train NOW he couldn't be back in time. He said, 'Jill, when *is* the party?'

'My party – Tuesday. It'll be paralysing but I'm counting on you all.'

'Not until Tuesday?' The earliest they could be back would be Thursday morning, three whole days late–

'You shall not be bored,' said Helmuth gaily, misunderstanding his dismay. 'These days Munich will be full of parades and parties and excitements–'

'Just like May week,' said Nick.

'Adolf himself will be in residence, and all the other big *bonzer.*' He glanced around before puffing his face up like a bullfrog's. 'And there will be the commemoration parades on Wednesday and the Bürgerbräukeller reunion and the ceremony of enrolling the new S.S. men–'

'Wasn't there something else?' Linné's voice was sarky as could be. 'Wasn't there another little party you promised us? Or have we forgotten that now?'

Helmuth said levelly, 'No, it is not forgotten. We will talk about it later.' He looked at his watch. 'I think we might now look for a glass of wine before we go to the Freiherr's.'

Once up and down the barrack street would be more than a kilometre. In the hour it would be possible to walk up and down three times. But exercise was something no one lacked. They drifted and eddied between the poplars, in small random movements, flapping green-grey figures starting to cluster together only to dissolve warily again into twos and threes, or individuals, even. Others, keeping a little apart, wore the blue and white stripes of the Jews. The smell of cigarettes and cigars was unnaturally acute in Emil's nose and – though he had never smoked, nor thought of smoking in his life – reassuring. So the smoke had smelled when the crowds drifted in the park at home on Sunday afternoon. His back hurt less when he walked than he'd expected though his legs were weak and he leaned without protest on the strong arm of the Brother who in the new vocabulary he now had to learn was also called the block-senior. For the moment he stopped feeling the jagged tooth with his

124

tongue, on whose tip the constant pricking had already raised a little blister.

The block-senior seemed well-known. Some of the bony brown faces they passed looked at him with deference, and not only those attached to bodies whose garb bore the violet badge of the Brethren. Once even a guard pedalling down the centre of the street on his great iron bicycle, the green-grey knots parting hurriedly to make way for him, shouted a coarse greeting. The block-senior was an older man, exactly how old the shapeless uniform and shaven head made hard to tell: perhaps as old as thirty. He was not there like Emil and most of the others in the block, simply for being a member of the society or refusing military service; he had been an active distributor of illegal literature, arrested with a suitcaseful of it in his possession, and had been in civil prison before being transferred to the KZ. After three years he was a veteran. He had taken charge of Emil as soon as Emil had been marched, half dragged, into the block after Initiation. Emil remembered little of the meeting now. Up to the flogging everything was vivid, in the right order: the last short rail journey, sitting on the wooden seat between two others, for the moment safe –

even normal, it could have been any crowded fourth-class compartment – looking out of the window at cabbage fields; slowing, stopping, starting again; clattering over points; a branch line curving away from the other tangle of lines and the terrible certainty that now the unknown was near; the train stopping finally but sitting there still, for a moment, quietly; squeezing his eyes shut and mouthing a prayer, oh such a prayer – then, as if to a familiar routine, a sudden explosion of shouts jerking everyone into action so that they jostled and pushed to leap down first on to the gravel, and straightway being chivvied and kicked through the gates and the random, meaningless blow that broke his tooth. Then lining up and standing stock still to be numbered and shouted at, the long table with the prison clerks scratching names and ages into ledgers, the place where you sat in a chair to face a camera and be photographed and when it was taken you jerked away from a stab in the bottom and looking down you saw the sharp point the photographer could cause to rise up, and heard a mirthless laugh from the guard who watched over, or standing again in naked shame – but his memory strove ahead, to the bare room

126

behind the big administration building that was still unfinished, and under a hanging electric bulb the wooden trestle…

The block-senior was asking, 'The other brother that came with thee, the farm-lad from Württemberg, that is allowed to lie on his bed today – he was first?'

'That is so.'

'On the trousers or was his person bared?'

'On the trousers when first a guard had smoothed them tight.'

'He received the five and twenty stripes?'

'Six and twenty, for they ordered him to count the blows himself and did not reckon the first a blow, for he had not then been ordered thus. After some number he could only utter a sound that was without sense but they accepted that.'

'He was offered the paper to sign?'

'Yes, after five blows, and refused.'

'Then it was thy turn?'

Emil nodded.

'Didst thou count the stripes?'

'The first was so unlike my expectation that I had not the breath. The other brother spoke for me, in a whisper.'

'Where was he?'

'On the floor where he had fallen' (on his hands and knees, his head also touching the ground, the seat of his trousers turning black with blood in the bare electric light).

'Thou wast also offered the paper?'

'After five blows, yes.'

'Thou saidst "No"?'

'My lips were large and bruised where I had bitten them and I could not say the word clearly–'

'But they took thy meaning?' The farm-boy had lifted and shaken his head too, like a dog, as if to encourage him. 'Thou didst not hesitate? They took thy meaning?' The block-senior's arm stiffened under Emil's.

'Without doubt.'

'Yet they laid no more stripes upon thee, only the five thou hadst already received?'

'That is so.'

'Thou undertook nothing?'

'Nothing.'

'Then why?–' The block-senior was anxious.

'They said–' but he could not repeat what the fatter guard had said, rubbing his hand coarsely over Emil's body as the other fluttered the paper– 'They said that I should think about the matter for some days. They said that since I now knew how five blows felt I should imagine how five times five would feel. They said I should have the twenty they owed me and twenty more besides.'

The block-senior took a dozen paces in silence. Then he asked, 'What was thy calling in the world?'

'I was apprenticed to the architect at Cannstadt.'

'Ah, yes.' The block-senior seemed suddenly satisfied. He said, 'It is not pleasant to await great hardship, knowing it will come. For the other brother perhaps it was easier. But the Lord in His power has seen that thou art keener here' – he tapped his bony head with his finger – 'than the brethren from farm or factory. Thou art less accustomed to pain. Thou needs more time to steel thy resolve. Thou wilt not falter, I know. "Thrice was I beaten with rods, once was I stoned" – Second Corinthians, ten, twenty-five.'

He took another dozen paces before adding, 'The Brethren are held in greater trust than any others here.'

Emil would have liked to ask by whom, but the block-senior continued proudly, 'The Commandant himself is shaved each morning by one of us. Many important duties in the camp are performed by Brethren. With thy skills it is possible there will be a place for thee in the works office. But first thou must show in everything thou art commanded that thou art not less industrious and trustworthy than those who have earned us this good name.'

'Wednesday it must be, then,' said Helmuth. Even here, in the walled garden of the vons and zus' house in the Mauer-Kircherstrasse he kept his voice low and darted suspicious glances into the glossy-leaved bushes. Lunch, which was duly a kind of stew with potatoes and dumplings and great knuckles of shiny bone, had passed off stiffly in the vons and zus' shabby dining-room and Pickup, observing no one much at ease save Helmuth, had found himself unexpectedly liberated from self-consciousness. The Freiherr was small and bald and held his head on one side and talked rapid, slurred German to everyone regardless of whether they understood him or not. The Freiin was small and fat and directed herself almost exclusively to poor Nick. The other girls were quiet at first, later began to murmur amongst themselves, though never giggling – looking up from his plate he'd sometimes caught the scrutiny of a pair, or two pairs of eyes which immediately flicked away again.

They came to a little summer house of stone and glass, some panes broken, in the farthest angle of the garden, hidden from the house by the shrubbery. *Moment!* Helmuth went across to a door set in the garden wall, opened it to peer into the quiet street outside and, reassured, led the way into the summer house. There were old cane chairs, an iron table, a broken terracotta urn, the parts of hammock seat and a faded archery target three feet or more in diameter.

'Once more, please, exactly what you propose.'

Philipp Linné told him, quickly, concisely. Pickup half-listened, still not really believing it, the rest of his attention vaguely trying to isolate, and identify, a low humming noise in his ears. For the time being he continued to loll in a cabbagey, complacent mood: Sunday afternoon felt reassuringly like Sunday afternoon anywhere else; heavy, inert – like nitrogen – to seep away as it liked. You expected nothing of it, so any pleasure that it might bring, a walk, a meeting, was nice and unexpected. If only Jill – she'd been animated at lunch as if (exceptionally for her) anxious that these four young men she'd lured from another world should make a good impression involving them all and suppressing those sharp, scoffing glosses she usually couldn't resist; but Jill had also announced with a casual directness that was more like herself that she had to go to a concert with Kurt, so if they liked to wait while she dashed off a letter to mummy and changed they could all go into the town together...

Kurt was a nephew of the vons and zus who'd been through an 'Order Castle,' which Jill said was a kind of martial public school, and was now an S.S. cadet out at Riem, due to be sworn in at this great ceremony Helmuth had mentioned. What about Helmuth? – wasn't it galling for him? But he had revealed nothing, only said affably, 'Then Nick and his friends, perhaps they would like to probe a bottle of good wine with me in the town.'

Helmuth was grumbling now, 'Wednesday is very soon. I cannot count on getting another message to Klaus by then.' He thought of something. 'But Wednesday is also very good: a special day, the officers will be preoccupied; at night they will be drinking and celebrating. Yes, yes – Wednesday is perhaps excellent!' He clapped Philipp Linné on the shoulder and wrung his hand, the dislike of the morning forgotten.

Pickup felt a sudden bump of confidence. Wednesday wasn't too bad. They could be back in Cambridge on Thursday. In seventy-two hours – no, less: seventy – they'd be safely on the train; in seven or eight safely out of the whole silly country, and the thing still ticking away. He let himself look forward passionately to the moment of release... He said, as they returned through the dank, still garden, 'What's that noise?'

'What noise? What do you mean?' Helmuth gripped his arm. His face had gone pale, actually gone pale, like in books – Pickup's optimism gurgled away.

'The humming noise. Can't you hear it?'

They all listened.

Helmuth said, 'Oh *that*. Dear Michael, you alarmed me. That is the Bayerische Moteren Werke – the B.M.W. factory, you know. When the wind is in the right quarter you may hear it all over the city.'

'But on Sunday afternoon?'

Helmuth laughed. 'On Sunday afternoon, on Sunday night, every night. It never stops.'

'Making cars?'

'Making engines. For our tanks, for our bombers, for our fighters that will puff your English bombers from the sky.'

They howled him down, so loudly that Helmuth put his finger to his lips but smiling his gold-toothed smile insisted, 'I tell you. They will, they will!'

## CHAPTER 5

Jackboots thrust apart, thumbs hooked into the leather belt round his brown tunic, the guard stood on top of the mountain of rubble shouting monotonously at the prisoners who toiled at its base, occasionally kicking a brick down the slope to land with a thud amongst, or against, them. If anyone were to flinch or pause in his work the guard would be down after it to lay about with his ox whip. One kept one's eyes down, picked and hacked and shovelled and waited for him to tire of being king of the castle, to descend with a random blow for someone on the way and mount his bicycle and ride away in search of fresh distraction, leaving only the gang-leader – shouting and cursing now, while the guard was present, but at other times not too mean a gang-leader: an old thief sent to the KZ for 're-education'.

Re-education indeed! One of the ironies Klaus Ihde had ceased to savour was that the department which indirectly had employed him at the university was also responsible for the camp.

He'd never been able to ingratiate himself enough with the Politicals who ran the works office to get a soft job: too aloof, too contemptuous at first. But at least he could now rely on being spared the worst of the labouring gangs, those in the stone quarry or the 'Plantation' or even – on this levelling task – the luckless detail whose members had to run with laden barrows to where the foundations for new barrack blocks were being laid and then back to this far northern corner of the camp area, exposed all the time to the attentions of passing guards...

The King of the Castle was on his way at last. Klaus Ihde closed his eyes, bracing himself for the blow, but it landed elsewhere. The gangleader screamed the party to attention. Only a commissioned officer rated that really, but flattery was an exact science in Dachau. Klaus resumed loading the barrow brought to him by the panting youth who wore the violet badge of the Bible Students. Something about him struck a chord. Was it of recognition, or only something imagined? There'd been a student once – well, one of many over the years – of whom he'd been fond, who had such an open, comical face with upturned nose and thick lips; of course, these lips were bruised and swollen, nor was there much that was comical now about the expression in the bible boy's eyes, hurt and fearful and already dulled in the way that only Dachau could dull. Yet he could not have been in long; his boots were new, his hands still small and soft, his complexion fresh. Klaus watched him struggling away with the loaded barrow, unaware that he might relax his desperation by a degree or two. He moved clumsily, as if unused to such labour, but beneath the shapeless clothes his body seemed well-made. Klaus felt a pang of compassion, the first since old Ehrlich had gone nearly three months before.

Pretending to be prising at a boulder of jagged cement and brick he manoeuvred himself to glance covertly in the other direction. The high wall of the camp rose only fifty metres away, shutting out all view of beyond – in a year all he'd seen of the outside world, hungrily, were the aircraft that sometimes flew across the sky above; the chimney sweep in top hat and blackened leather who a month before had been escorted carefully round the camp by an armed guard; and the Katro van from Munich bringing in canteen supplies. He'd wheedled his way into the band of volunteers who helped with the unloading on Saturday afternoons in the hope of a cup of coffee – actual coffee! And some weeks back had felt palmed into his hand the first of these messages, on a scrap of squared paper; a later one was pencilled inside a tattered copy of the *Volkischer Beobachter* the canteen orderly with the potato-nose had offered him with a grunt. Could he trust them? He applied himself to filling the barrow brought by an old Jew whose cheeks were sucked in horribly as he wheezed for breath. Klaus gave him a week to go. Probably not even that. But how much longer for himself? He had started to notice a puffiness in his legs, a bad sign; there was a sore on his arm from which he squeezed more pus every night: he had pyorrhoea.

He studied the perimeter again: within the outer wall was another lower one, then the water-filled ditch, then the electric fence; in the front of that the strip, six metres wide, to venture on which meant instant execution. At the populated end of the camp it had been planted with grass. But here, at this corner far from the nearest barrack block, it had only been roughly cleared. Here, too, was the last demolition site in the camp, to afford some concealment on a dark night, perhaps even some useful aids ... the building had been part of an old powder factory; he'd come across some interesting old machinery; also a great crock – for acid, presumably – which would have delighted friend Ehrlich; it had been smashed up and sent on its way with the bricks and stones and lumps of cement to make the foundations for barracks 27 and 28. There were timber beams, and, most significantly, a length of ladder which had once led to the loft and which, pretending to lug it aside one misty morning when the gang leader was cuffing a Jew, he had managed to drop into a patch of weeds which had accepted and concealed it, at least until the frosts came to wither them.

Here, too, one was farthest from a machine gun tower, nearly 300 metres, for they were spaced more widely away from the barracks. Finally, quite close – sometimes one could hear the sound of a lorry, or a car horn – ran the main Prittlbach road. Crude maps of the environs circulated in the camp and were acquired by hopefuls who cherished ideas of one day breaking away from an outside working party. One man had actually succeeded during a blizzard the previous winter, only to be recaptured within a few days and paraded, already half-dead, round the camp before disappearing into the punishment bunker, never again to be seen. Well, that was escape, too, in the end. Perhaps the only real escape from Dachau: slowly, destroyed by pain, hanging by your thumbs from a meathook or pounded on the block until a kidney ruptured; with luck, quickly, from a bullet or the jolt of a thousand volts from the wire – would one feel anything at all that way? In theory it sounded the easiest quietus. He had thought of making that last act of affirmation often enough. Every morning the spirit quailed on waking to another day. But survive, survive! The life-urge still faintly pulsed. The mysterious escape plan was perhaps the logical course. If it was unlikely to succeed, with luck it would at least end abruptly. And, like Pascal wagering on the existence of God, what had he to lose?

The Third Secretary said, 'Very well, I will come down.' From behind her typewriter

Frau Ochs gave him a reproachful look. If the work of the embassy was to be interrupted every time some insignificant person presented himself at the door and demanded to see the Ambassador, nothing would ever be accomplished. The Third Secretary, very young and slim and straight, followed the porter along the corridor and down the big curving staircase to the main hall. Frau Ochs bent her head to her work, dating the letter she had just begun to type, Paris, November 7th, 1938. The busy click-clack of the keys almost obscured the sound of the pistol shot from below.

From the roof truss was suspended an Albatross D.VIII fighter from the war, not just a model but the actual plane, glowing crimson, black Maltese crosses boldly emphasised with a white edging; at the far end of the hall a queue of school-children shuffled slowly up the ladderway to the corrugated fuselage – and one wing – of a Junkers transport. If they had to kill this time in Munich the Deutsche Museum, especially the Transport section, was as good a place as any. The wild proposition had even crossed Pickup's mind that he might make out a case to the college that he filled his time in Munich studying heat engines. Take back lots of notes, buy some German text-books, that was it – even as he worked out the thought he knew it was vain.

'Come on, Mickup,' Nicholson was looking back impatiently. 'We're supposed to meet Phil in half an hour.'

'Let's just see the Zepps.' There was another hanging exhibit beckoning, a model this time but a big one: a Zeppelin with a section of the fabric omitted to reveal the framework beneath. 'I say, how about that for a structure? Weren't airships marvellous? I was taken as a kid to Cardington, to see the R.100 or R.101, not sure which–'

But Nicholson was already making for the *Ausgang*.

Emil took the can of water and swallowed it greedily. His mouth was dry and salty. He handed the can back to the water-carrier, who swore indeterminedly at him and moved off towards the next gang. The prisoner who had been helping him load his barrow said, 'In summer when you are parched they taunt you, make you grovel for a drink. But in winter when you don't need it they're keen enough to keep their nice little job going.'

141

'But they are also prisoners.'

The man laughed. 'You expect brotherly love, brother?'

Emil saw: a thin face with thin lips sharply defined, bright eyes and even through the grime and dust, bright spots of colour beneath the cheekbones; a short, slight frame; when he opened his mouth, yellowed teeth. He heard: an educated, unexpectedly melodious voice that for the first time since his arrest used the courtesy second-person *Sie*.

He replied likewise, 'You see my badge.'

The man nodded his head, then looked sharply up at Emil. 'Were you not one of the bible students called out for punishment two nights ago?'

He hesitated. 'I was.'

'You recovered very quickly.'

He hesitated again. 'I had but five lashes.'

'I thought it was twenty-five.'

'I have the others to come, also as many again, they said.'

The man looked grave. 'That is not an easy prospect to bear.'

'The block-senior, who is also a Brother, said that I am chosen to bear it.'

'And can you?'

Emil's lips quivered. He looked away in

confusion. 'I must.'

The man laid a hand on his arm like a bird alighting. 'Then your God be with you.'

The clatter of boots, shouts, exploded on Pickup's ears. He thought, It's all up, and desperately prayed, *Oh please God* – he saw black figures ringing Ian Nicholson and Linné, and Linné's hat dashed to the ground. He stopped where he was. There was a red face turning towards him, staring accusingly from under a steel helmet. He pursed his lip, pretending to remember something he'd forgotten, pretending he was nothing to do with THEM. He took half a dozen steps, looked irresolutely back... He'd been lagging behind, dreaming, a bit disgruntled, as they drifted from the Odeonsplatz past the Feldherrnhalle memorial – of course! Linné must have done what they'd been warned against a million times, forgotten – or even refused, knowing him – to raise his hat to the dead. Why did he want to wear a hat, the silly idiot? He glanced back: the S.S. men stood in their same menacing ring. He saw Linné gesticulating, even heard his voice. Nicholson stood stock still, a little apart. Passers-by hurried on their way not stopping to look.

He found himself by, and entered, the

alley which by-passed the Feldherrnhalle. Helmuth had shown it them once, making a little joke about how many Müncheners seemed to prefer the 'Umwegstrasse' to passing the memorial. When he regained the street and looked back the tableau had dissolved; the others were coming away, Linné holding the crumpled hat stiffly at his side.

In the hotel room he was still quivering with – what? Rage? Fear? It was hard to say. He kept saying, 'The thugs, the ignorant thugs, who the *hell* do they think they are?'

'It wasn't a very clever thing to do,' said Nicholson. He'd positioned himself by the door, as if trying to blanket Linné's protestations with his body. 'How would you like it if someone cocked a snook at the Cenotaph?'

'But that is a proper War Memorial, to a million who died. A farcical revolution, some of whose poor fools contrived to get themselves shot – that's not quite the same thing. Did you ever read an account of the Putsch?'

'For God's sake keep your voice down.'

Nick, coming in from a birthday shopping expedition with Jill, had to be told the story, and roared with laughter.

'I wish you'd take this whole damned business more seriously,' said Linné. 'It's not just a lark, you know.'

*Lark* was another word that on his lips had a foreign sound.

'If it's not, then why are we doing it?'

'What do you mean?'

'What other motive can we possibly have, than doing it for fun?'

'For fun?'

'For the sake of doing it, then.'

Linné stared at him in hostility and disbelief.

Pickup tried to change the subject. 'You should have seen the Germans, hurrying by pretending not to notice.'

'I didn't see you exactly rushing to the rescue,' said Nicholson. 'Quite a study in discretion as the better part of valour from our Mickup.'

'What would have been the good of the three of us getting nabbed?' he said hotly. 'Supposing they hadn't let you go – I was going to go to the Consul or somewhere.'

'Quite right,' said Linné unexpectedly. 'It was the only sensible thing to do. But what would Nick have done? Laughed his head off? Come on, Nick, what is all this to you?

Is it no more than another joke? For if so–'

Nick said, 'Don't be boring, Linnaeus' – Linnaeus was a nickname like Mickup for Pickup but one that had never really caught on.

Linné said, 'Look, Nick, you are our leader – at least in the sense that we exist around you. You are the nucleus. I want to know what you feel about – well, about the camp. Does it anger you, or is it just a place to exercise your ingenuity?'

'According to the posters they've got stuck up everywhere we had them first, in South Africa.'

'You believe that to be true?'

'It wouldn't surprise me.'

'All right. Then this man Ihde: you feel nothing about him? No concern of any kind?'

Nick said lightly, 'How can I feel anything about someone I never met? Especially when he's–'

'Especially when he's what?'

'You know.'

'A homosexual, you are saying? What the Nazis smeared him with.'

'Well, even Helmuth admitted there were lots of jokes about him. Those tutes when they'd go in the woods and take their clothes off to be like Greek youth. Can you imagine them? – throwing the javelin and things, bollocko!' He laughed even more loudly. Pickup felt a twinge of disloyalty.

Linné flopped down on one of the beds. He said, 'And for that he should be held without trial, beaten, tortured? – you heard the old man in London, didn't you?' His voice rose.

Nicholson said, 'For the last time, keep it quieter, everyone.' Then: 'Listen, Philipp, just because we don't get waxy about everything it doesn't mean we don't care. You should know what the English are like by now.'

Linné flushed, the first time Pickup had ever seen him do so. He said, 'I'm sorry. I was forgetting–'

There was silence for a moment.

Nick said, 'How did you get on at the works?'

'There was no problem. I made myself known again, threw my weight about, rummaged in that fool Ristow's files while he was out of his office, sowed the idea that we might want to borrow a motor-van...'

'I saw Helmuth, by the way. He was taking July to a tea-dance. He's sent the message. For 10 p.m., Wednesday.'

'Good,' said Linné. 'What else did he say?'

'Nothing much. Mostly he was full of some Hun who's been shot in the embassy in Paris – I've forgotten the name.'

'Dead?' said Nicholson.

'I don't think so. The point is he was shot by a Jew. Helmuth didn't know whether to be enraged or anxious – he thinks there's bound to be trouble.'

Linné had rolled back his left sleeve. The smooth tanned skin of his forearm was almost encircled by a bruise. He said 'You know what that thug called me? You heard, Ian, didn't you? He called me a dirty Jew.'

Between supper and Lights Out the latrine became the social centre of the block. Those who weren't using, or waiting to use, the big glazed brown lavatories, eight in a row, stood and smoked and talked and speculated. Klaus Ihde, washing his yellow teeth at the adjoining circular wash-basin round which – in the morning – as many as fifteen men would jostle together, was probably the only one who still noticed, and inwardly wrinkled his nose, at the stench of smoke and excreta.

Tonight the talk was all of the shooting of the diplomat vom Rath in Paris, The news had spread like wildfire through the camp from half a dozen sources. An old Political who had a job as a servant in an officer's household said the officer's wife had called him to hear the news on the radio himself. At evening roll-call it had been noticed that the guards were even more vicious than usual towards the Jews, for it was said that a Jew had done the deed – calling at the embassy, cool as you please, asking to see the ambassador and when vom Rath came down to see him, pulling out a gun and firing... There was endless speculation as to what might happen if the diplomat died. Voices said, they would not be in the Jews' skins for anything; others, the Jews only asked for trouble if this is what a Jew would do...

Ihde spat into the basin and reached up to the central tap to flush away the pink spittle from his sore, spongy gums. Poor Jews, they were in for a bad time – but even as his mind expressed the sentiment for him it was ticking off the possible advantages in the situation: if more attention for the Jews, less for everyone else, since even the illiterate apes of the S.S. were governed by simple mathematics; there were thirty of them to six thousand prisoners. If really large-scale reprisals against Jewry, then perhaps they'd actually have to release some other categories to make room ... ah, was that just a wish-fantasy? Dachau was ever full of fantasies. Once the Reich was completed and the last oppressed folk in Slovakia and Poland gathered in, then a great amnesty, save for the Jews; or if war came, the same; or the 'good' sturmbanfuhrer with the aristocratic name who disdained brutality and had once been observed to wipe his boots before entering a barrack – he would become commandant and overnight all would be changed...

But there was a tension in the camp that could not be denied, a feeling that something might be happening. On evening roll-call the signal that they were at last to be dismissed was when the light in the commandant's office went out; but tonight it had stayed burning as they doubled away from the square. On top of this situation he, Klaus Ihde, had in his pocket, until such time as the crowd thinned when he might shred it and flush the pieces away, yet another cryptic message handed to him, inside a packet of cigarette papers, by the old sweat from the canteen. It confirmed the date, the time, indicated a place – not knowing that to a protective captive in KZ Dachau the date could be as remote and undivinable as the weather in Madrid. Even if you spent precious pfennigs on the Volkischer *Beobachter* from the canteen you couldn't be sure it wasn't a day or two old. Fortunately the vom Rath news afforded a point of reference, the sacred date of November 9th another – a pleasing coincidence that it should also be the date set by those who signed themselves simply, Your Friends.

Was it a trap? But who needed to trap a man already broken in body and mind and spirit, decaying where he stood, preserved only in one dark, scheming corner of his being ...? If only he were young and strong, what hope would flame within him. Perhaps an accomplice! – that poor, stupid, touching young Bible-bug who still moved like a boy, who was trembling at what was in store for him, had no lack of incentive. Dare he share with him the secret? Well, the brethren were famous for their trustworthiness. They also had this dour satisfaction at being oppressed. It might be that his beliefs forbad him to evade his portion. To think that he himself had once debated the ethics of escape with the good gaunt Ehrlich. What had he argued again? Something about affirmation. Words,

words, words. The only realities were the sore on his leg, his gums, his wedge of bread, his two blankets and the stink around him.

## CHAPTER 6

In the splintered light of chandeliers the vons and zus' house had magically lost its dinginess. The servant who took their coats wore silver-buttoned livery over a yellow-striped waistcoat; from behind the tall double doors came thin sounds of music. Pickup, who'd set out confident and joking with the others felt an onset of gawkiness. Within the picture room an unfamiliar Jill was formally receiving the guests, watchfully flanked by the vons and zus. To the grey-haired officer who'd arrived just ahead of them she smiled, bobbed and extended her hand as she'd extended it – how many ages ago? – to that gaunt tramp in the basement in Chelsea, but the instant he had gravely kissed it, clicked his heels and made to move on, flashed to her brother and the rest of them a grimace so extravagantly aghast that Pickup heard Nicholson, of all people, snort with laughter. Another instant and she was the aspirant hostess again. It was her hair that was different, Pickup saw, curled and crimped by some Munich hairdresser into tight, unlovely waves. Her shoulders were bare, densely patterned with freckles which shaded away and then disappeared altogether from the creamy swell above her low-cut dress–

'Michael,' she murmured, 'God, what a dank occasion. It's super of you all to have come all this way.' With the wink she gave him went a squeeze of his hand. Pickup moved on thinking, the others hadn't had that, had they? But as he glanced back there was Helmuth, the starched white front of his dress shirt enriching his tan and even the vons and zus fluttering with pleasure at the arrival of their favourite. And already within the room, already dominating it despite holding himself to respectful attention to talk to the grey officer, he who was of course the S.S. cadet Kurt: about twenty, he supposed, unsmiling in a black uniform buttoned high, erect, lean-featured, a bit like Nicholson except – as they drew nearer – a curiously petulant, almost feminine softness about the mouth which Nicholson certainly didn't have; more like Linné, in fact.

The other girls were ranged methodically in a half circle, fans or little bead purses in hand, some talking to young men who'd already arrived, the remaining four or five eyeing the newcomers curiously. The older guests – Jill had complained that the vons and zus used these parties, subsidised by parents, to keep up their own entertaining – had collected together, gossiping in low voices. Another servant circulated with a tray of champagne in tall fluted glasses.

Pickup found himself appropriated by a mousy girl from Roumania who tackled him accusingly in French and then doggedly in English. Yes, it was a long way to come for a party but it was up to one to show the flag, wasn't it? No, he had regrettably never been to Bucharest. Yes, Munich was a lovely city and its museums were indeed interesting...

Jill was with Nick and Helmuth and vons and zus, more informally now, with champagne glasses in their hands, and as Pickup looked Nick's bray of laughter rang out, but the vons and zus were still shooting glances at the door and obviously anxious not to let the reception arrangements break up altogether.

Pickup excused himself from the mousy girl and hovered on the outskirts of the little group that had now formed round the S.S. cadet. He talked in clipped, harsh German with a frequent trick of jerking his jaw forward as if – Pickup guessed – to harden that too-plump profile. Linné muttered a low running translation to Nicholson and the cadet, aware of this, would pause considerately between sentences to let the interpreter catch up. '...After the first year it was not so – er – arduous. We had done all the marches and drilling and tough-guy stuff. But now one had to work even harder on the – er – military science and philosophy...' Nicholson listened attentively but his eyes never left the cadet's face.

A girl broke in, her voice light and inconsequential after the cadet's. He nodded gravely and replied. Linné: 'Yes, and tomorrow at midnight all is ... fulfilled, or rewarded perhaps, when he is inducted as an officer–'

The girl's voice again, and the reply which needed no translation. 'Well, you heard that – by Reichsminster Hess himself, at the Feldherrnhalle.'

Pickup was aware the cadet was staring at him questioningly. Linné introduced him with a phrase he recognised as 'another friend from England.' The German continued to stare at him. Pickup felt it was up to him to say something. He said without thinking much, 'Shouldn't you be keeping some sort of vigil tonight?' The cadet frowned incomprehendingly. 'I mean, in the old orders of chivalry the what-do-you-call-him – the candidate – would stay up all night in prayer or meditation. There was a soulful picture in all the history books.'

Nicholson was glaring at him but Linné translated with a shrug and a half-smile. The cadet's eyes hardened. Then he also shrugged and spoke. Linné said, 'He says the knight of the Schutzstaffeln keeps an eternal vigil.'

As the group broke up Nicholson hissed, 'For the last time, these wet jokes of yours are going to get us all into trouble.'

Linné murmured, 'It's all right. Once he'd made his mind up that his leg wasn't being pulled he was quite pleased ... knight of the S.S. indeed! They're about as chivalrous as baboons.' He spat out the last word with such vehemence that Pickup flinched, sure that everyone would hear and understand, but Linné went on, 'It gets more hopeful all the time. Tomorrow, I mean. It's obviously the great S.S. day, and given some luck they will be preoccupied by it to the exclusion of almost everything.'

There was a stir from the other end of the room. The vons and zus' last anxiously-awaited guest had arrived. They fussed behind Jill as she received him, the Freiherr wringing his hands, the Freiin sharply beckoning the servant with the wine, then all accompanying the guest as he stormed purposefully towards the buffet and the crowd of older people, who arranged them-selves into a respectful semi-circle. He was thickly-built, coarse-featured, in a black double-breasted suit with party badge prominent on the lapel, from the Bavarian Minister-President's department, Pickup knew; not one of the real big-shots but something of a catch for the dowdy vons and zus, even if he wasn't in evening dress. Helping himself to chicken and sausage and tiny mushrooms impaled on wooden sticks Pickup listened as general pleasantries died away and the minister delivered himself of a monologue to much head-shaking and lip-pursing. The grey-haired officer broke in, the minister droned on, drank some cham-pagne, accepted a cigar from the Freiherr, and seemed to brighten, his audience dutifully brightening too.

Helmuth, who had been standing on the

fringe of the semi-circle, sauntered away. He linked an arm in Pickup's and led him to join Jill. He said, 'The news from Paris is not so good. Vom Rath, you know–'

'Dead?'

'Not yet. Do not hurry the poor chap. But there is not so much hope, it seems. The minister says he is anxious it should not spoil tomorrow's events. November the ninth is always an important day for Munich.'

'What does he mean, he hopes the vom Rath business won't spoil it?'

'I don't know.' Helmuth seemed uneasy.

Jill tugged towards them another man whom Pickup had vaguely noticed on the edge of the crowd round the minister. She said, 'Hey, you *must* meet the Consul-General.'

The Consul-General shook their hands and now you looked at him he was very English and mild, rather like Pickup's father, Pickup thought, and about the same age, but with a certain watchfulness about him. He said, 'Good gracious, how many more of you? All this way for Miss Amering's party – that's certainly a demonstration of loyalty.' He looked from Nick to Pickup and back to Nick. 'Are you all up at Cambridge?'

Nick nodded.

'And no trouble about getting an exeat in mid-term? They were pretty strict in my day, I seem to remember.'

'This is rather a special occasion.'

'We're going first thing tomorrow,' said Pickup.

Jill asked, 'How's Louise?'

'Oh, very well except for being hit in the eye playing lacrosse.'

'Did you meet Louise in the summer, Nick? She's the Consul's daughter. At school. Comes for the holidays–'

'I don't think so,' said Nick.

'And hates it here,' pursued Jill.

The Consul replied equably, if lowering his voice a fraction. 'She's perhaps a little sensitive. Says she finds the atmosphere rather ... upsetting.'

'Gosh, crossing the frontier on the train–' Pickup pulled himself up, unsure whether he should finish the sentiment,

The Consul said, 'And how do you find it, Miss Amering?'

She tilted her head. 'There's no wrapping paper in the shops, the Weisswurst tastes like blotting paper, the coffee's foul and the silk stockings don't last five minutes.'

'That's not quite what I meant.'

'Oh, otherwise it's ... well, when I go home

England feels half dead. Here they make things happen.'

The Consul nodded, consulted his pocket-watch, seemed about to go, then looked first Nick in the eye, then Pickup, and added, 'By the way, if you have a moment do look in at the office. Miss Amering knows where it is – in the Prannerstrasse. We like to keep in touch.'

'Actually we're off in the morning,' said Pickup again.

'What did he say to you?' asked Linné afterwards.

Nick told him. Pickup added, 'He wondered how we got permission from the college.'

Nicholson said, 'God, you're not still worrying about *that*, are you?'

Linné said, 'Actually, it would not be a bad idea if he *were* expecting a call from us in the morning – just in case.'

'With any luck he won't get one.'

'I know, but no harm in making sure you can find him if you do have to. Ask him if he'd be free at eleven-thirty.'

The older guests were settling to talk or play cards, or taking their leave. From the picture room came the sound of the little band striking up again. The younger ones

160

moved in to dance.

*In London Rolf Ehrlich approached the end of his account.*

My release from Dachau was as sudden as it was unexpected. Although the arrival of so many Austrians had eventually forced a number of releases, the authorities had also sought to ease the overcrowding by the transfer of prisoners to another camp. Since this other camp enjoyed a notoriety even greater, if possible, than Dachau's, there was little consolation here. Those who did get release were chiefly criminals or members of the 'work-shy' category and – it was observed – of an age and strength such that they might yet provide the State with some useful skill or muscle-power, plus those Jews upon whose behalf relatives had been able to obtain a visa to a foreign country. In most cases such a prisoner also owned property in the Reich which he agreed to forfeit to the State.

I seemed to qualify for neither category. I should here explain that which I hoped not to explain, that my daughter's husband, while not an influential member of the Party – had he been I might have been free much

161

sooner, for bribery and favouritism thrive in the Reich – was nevertheless a keen Nazi. To spare her confusion I had deliberately avoided communication with my daughter, save for a brief note after my arrest urging her to forget me. Of course the dear girl had insisted on writing, and even sending the RM 15 which each prisoner was permitted to receive a month. What I did not know was that she had also approached a business man in Belgium with whom I had dealt for many years. Through this man's efforts and, no doubt, some customary 'greasing of the machinery' both my release and a temporary visa to Belgium were obtained. From Belgium, through the good offices of the Society whose name I bless but should not reveal, I was able to proceed in due course to England.

My number was called among some thirty others over the camp loudspeaker, ordering us at once to the administrative office. Such summons had been occurring for some days and by now were known to mean release or transfer rather than the punishment they threatened in ordinary times, so it was with hope tempered mainly by disappointment that K. had not also been called that I ran across the great square. 'What do you want, you?' – 'Protective captive number—respectfully reports in answer to the loud-speaker announcement, Herr Storm-troop-leader.'

Was it to be transfer or release? The particularly ranting tone of voice of the officer and the guards gave us the answer at once. The prospect of returning a prisoner still alive to the outside world seemed to produce in them a resentment which K., when I told him of it, decided must be due to the realisation that their conduct was soon to be viewed from a civilised vantage point – within the camp the most bestial deeds had long ceased to be regarded as anything but normal. At the same time they sought by a final display of intimidation to prevent released prisoners, especially those that were to remain in the country, from talking about their experiences. This made the last hours in the camp peculiarly fraught because to suffer a mark on the body at this stage, from a boot or whip, would – as I shall explain – have been disastrous.

In my case they contented themselves with remarks that the Reich would be well served by the departure of such traitors. K. on the other hand hailed it as great victory for the principles and aims of survival he had worked out. His joy was all the more affecting when one perceived the agony of disappointment that lay beneath it. Bravely he pretended that his turn would not be long in coming; after all he had arrived three months after I had, and it often seemed to be a year's ordeal. I feigned encouragement of this view. We both knew that Politicals, as he was classed, had the smallest prospect of release; moreover, he had no relatives other than an aged mother. The last night we braved the threats of the block-senior and talked until a late hour. I made him promise to continue the struggle for the preservation of his personality. He made me swear in return that on reaching freedom I would before anything else write down all I could remember of the most hateful place on earth and endeavour to publish it to the world. This, to the limit of my poor ability, I now attempt.

Next morning, with the other fortunate ones, I faced Dachau's final rituals. We stood naked before the infirmary block until the S.S. doctor came out to inspect us for wounds or other marks that might betray what took place in the camp – one poor Jew whose wrists still bore the signs of the tree was rejected and moaned so pitiably that he soon collected bruises to postpone his release for many days to come. We took a hot shower and received back our former clothes, which in nearly all cases hung loosely upon the wearer. We listened to a speech from the deputy commandant, praising the Nazi State and threatening us with instant re-arrest should we offend it in any way and in particular if we should describe our experiences to anyone. We signed receipts for our goods, whether all were returned or not. We signed a document declaring we had not been ill-treated and had no claim against the State. We signed for a sum of RM 15 and a third-class railway ticket as far as Munich. We formed into a little column and marched out under the gate that bore the legend 'Work Makes Free' and through the S.S. barracks. We marched the three kilometres to Dachau station. The guards accompanying us shouted and cursed no less than before. We waited on the station apart from the other passengers. We boarded the train and sat in silence, one guard remaining with us to make sure we talked to no one. At Munich he remained, arms akimbo, on the platform as we moved towards the exit, still silent, fearful, separate, the spaces between us widening, waiting to hear his savage recall, incredulous when it did not come and now walking ever faster, dispersing in the manner of electrically charged particles that repel each other.

Now that he was dancing with her at last, after Kurt and Helmuth and Nick and the Freiherr, even, and Kurt again, had all danced with her, he couldn't think of anything to say. Her hair was stiff against his face and he breathed the heady pong of whatever the hairdresser had put on it. Her dress was backless as well as low-cut and when he held her with extra tightness in a turn his thumb and forefinger actually touched flesh which was bare and cool and springy–

'Oops, sorry!'

And a minute later: 'You have the nicest feet I've ever trodden on.'

She said with a shrug he could feel, 'You're not as bad as Nick, anyway.'

'Helmuth's a jolly good dancer, isn't he?' He was fishing for some sign that Helmuth was still the one she was going with really, because Helmuth was nice and, more important, Helmuth was non-disturbing. You couldn't think of him as a real rival but while he was about there was no need to compete: the only snag was that it was the sinister Kurt she'd danced with twice, who she'd been out with on Sunday evening, who could sense – whenever they passed near him – was the one she was prickling towards.

He tried again: 'Did you hear about the fracas at the Feldherrnhalle – or whatever it is?'

She made a little snort – half of amusement, half exasperation. 'Honestly, you should have more sense, Philipp especially. An English boy at the University got his glasses smashed the other day.'

What should his attitude be? Indignant at such tough-guy stuff? Or just amused? Or uncritically admiring? It was too late for that now, unless as a bluff. He said, 'How did you meet whatsisname – Kurt?'

'Oh, with a crowd. It was an ice-hockey match when the Canadians came over. Everyone was cheering the Germans on, so I cheered the Canadians. Kurt was astonished, he'd assumed I was German. You know, blonde hair, Nordic profile.'

'Did he really say that?'

'Not in as many words, but – yes.'

'They're quite dotty about things like that, aren't they?'

Again that shrug.

He said suddenly, recklessly, 'You remember when we went swimming that day?' And managing to bluff a little, 'Where was it? Began with a D...'

Without expression: 'Dachau.'

'That was it. Well, that camp thing we saw afterwards – you know, those terrible walls, and the people we told you about that we saw at the station that night – what does he think about that? The S.S. are in charge there, aren't they?'

'Haven't you forgotten Helmuth's friend who's supposed to be inside the place? We mustn't forget him.' With vehemence, *'Of course* it's bloody, but ... God, do we have to talk about it now?'

'I'm sorry.'

I have several times been asked since arriving in this country, how much do my fellow-Germans know of what is going on in the concentration camps? As I mentioned when I began these notes I myself in the summer of 1937 had seen only non-committal references in the German Press. Word of mouth rumours circulated, however, and when it suits their purpose the Nazi journals are now more open about the existence and purpose of the camps. The disgusting anti-Jewish cartoons in *Der Stürmer*, for instance, will sometimes depict Jews in forced labour situations. I have been told, though I did not see it myself, that a representational road sign of the type that is popular in Germany indicates the direction of Dachau by the device of an S.S. man hauling a Jew by his hair. There was sometimes debate amongst us in the camp as to the particular responsibility to be borne by the citizens of the town of Dachau. Some prisoners who had been outside the camp on working parties said that they had received sympathetic looks and even drinks or food from the locals. Others said that they saw only eyes averted. Some claimed that the burghers resented the existence of the camp and treated the S.S. with coldness; others that the town prospered as a result of their presence. K., who had known Dachau in happier days when it was a favourite haunt of artists, insisted that painters still had their easels set up within a kilometre of the roll-call square while on fine Sundays families would be taking their afternoon walk outside the very walls of the camp.

For myself I cannot believe that my countrymen really understand what is happening behind those walls. I will go further and say no people on earth would accept the establishment of a detention camp where it was announced that citizens might be held indefinitely without trial, where savage punishments could be inflicted at the whim of a junior officer, where murder and torture were everyday occurrences, where more than 10 per cent of the inmates would not survive a year. But of course no such announcement was ever made in Germany, nor – in the absence of a free Press – could such information be obtained or published independently. More important, at no time could it be said that Dachau, anyway, was being deliberately set up in the shape I have described. When it was first instituted in 1933 the object was to confine those obvious and immediate adversaries of the N.S.D.A.P. in the years before the coming to power, the Communists and trade-unionists, and prevent them from working or speaking against the new regime. There may even have been a small core of truth in the declared aim to 're-educate' these men by work and discipline. *Arbeit Macht Frei* runs the legend over the entrance gate – 'Work leads to freedom.'

Gradually the categories of prisoners

admitted were extended to include other 'enemies' of the State: churchmen, both Catholic and Evangelist, who preached too openly against Nazi doctrine; the luckless Bible students; liberals like my dear friend K; those like myself who were suspected of betraying the State or of not working hard enough for it. Gradually the camp also became the place for those groups who did not 'fit in' to the National Socialist ideal: the gypsies and tinkers and of course the Jews. And gradually the routine of the camp became more and more inhuman. If the young men who are the guards had been instructed at the beginning to treat the prisoners as they do, I believe it is likely that many would have been unable to comply for even the Party stormtroopers who fought with the Communists in the years before 1933, rough and violent as they were, did not strike me as being coldly cruel.

Cruelty does not spring naturally into men's hearts. It is the product of callousness and contempt; it grows and hardens and grows again wherever these attitudes are encouraged. Each generation of S.S. men posted to the camp inherits the traditions of those who had gone before and 'improves' upon them. In the same way the acceptance of the camps by the rest of the population becomes more and more difficult to resist, for at which point should the people cry 'Halt' even if they suspect what is being done? If they did not object to the disappearance of the gypsies – and it must be admitted that the gypsies were often dirty, and littered the beauty of the land, and stole from farms and houses – how should they object to the disappearance of the Jews?

Posters in Germany seek to avert criticism of Dachau and other places by claiming that it was the British who invented concentration camps in a colonial war and administered them with a barbarity far removed from the 'educational' firmness of the German camp. I cannot comment on this statement, but as I related earlier I heard many accounts during my military service of field prisons whose arduous drills and summary punishments were not so different from accounts I was later to hear of the early days in Dachau. Recently, walking by a barracks in London, I chanced to observe one who was obviously a soldier in detention being hurried across the square between two other soldiers. His gait and the loose, ill-fitting overalls he wore gave me an unpleasant shock of recognition.

I say that any country which has a military prison or a reform school for the young where military drills are part of the 'correction' and can find the staff to operate such places, has also the germ of a future Dachau. Ah! The reader will object, but in our democracies the germ would never be allowed to grow. Our safeguards of Parliament, a free Press and a judiciary system aloof from the State would soon warn us of the danger and protect us from it. I fervently agree, and weep for my poor country that it should have so unresistingly surrendered these safeguards. I still maintain that in every country there are to be found some envious and sick and unsuccessful men ready to act as oppressors and torturers. Have I not read in England that every day applications are received for the position of public hangman? I would still remind the good democrat that every time he thoughtlessly says: 'Oh, I wish we could get rid of these dirty gypsies,' or 'Oh, these strikers should be locked up,' he is asking for a concentration camp.

I must return from philosophic musings for which I am ill-equipped to the grim reality of Dachau, where the germ is now five years old. I have tried to give some idea of how it has grown in that time. Now I am haunted by the question how will it *continue to grow?* The extension of existing camps and the construction of new ones cannot keep pace with the ever increasing numbers of those condemned to them. The number of releases is trifling by comparison. For the Jews who constitute a greater and greater proportion of the 'Protective Captives' release is considered only when emigration has been offered. I will not here enter the controversy over the restrictions which this country and the other free countries of the world place upon the number of 'refugees' they will accept. I ask only that the dreadful plight of those that remain will be remembered in the council chambers of democracy. I lie awake at night tormented by the fear that in these dark places where death is already a by-product it may one day become the deliberate aim.

They danced once again. She seemed sweeter, more yielding this time, perhaps because the party had soon to end. Even her hair was softer on his cheek. Pickup couldn't be sure it was actually the Last Waltz, which at the parish hall hops at home was when they put the lights down and it was the accepted thing to be a bit smoochy, but people were certainly beginning to go. Nicholson had been signalling impatiently for the last quarter of an hour and now he and Phil Linné were standing stiffly to make their farewells to the vons and zus. He'd dreaded this moment above all others, the party being over and the flatness he'd feel at the best of times made a hundred times worse by the imminence of what came next – and yet, now it was here he felt light-headed. For the first time he'd been almost gay with her, in the way he always saw himself. He needed only something senti-mental to take away.

He said, 'It's like the Waterloo Ball.'

'What do you mean?'

'Everyone being called away to Do their Duty.'

'I don't see.'

'Well, Kurt has to go and keep his vigil. We have to–'

'Have to what?'

There was a tension to her voice. Did she wonder, did she care about him? He said lightly, 'Get back.'

She pushed back against his encircling arm so as to look up into his eyes. She said, 'Michael, Nick's been a bit funny all evening. Are you up to something?'

An urge to tell her everything welled up in him. Oh, to feel her admiration and concern, to drop the foppish mask of Sir Percy and stand forth as the Scarlet Pimpernel! But instead he held her tightly again and let his lips brush recklessly against her brow.

## CHAPTER 7

Pickup lay warmly half-awake for a moment, letting himself sink cosily back into sleep ... then remembered sickeningly what day it was. He opened his eyes. The room was still dark, the ornate top of the wardrobe only a darker blur against the general blur. He heard the ticking of Nick's watch but no sound of breathing. He peeped again: the long lump in the next bed was motionless; perhaps he was lying sleepless. The lump stirred and exhaled. Pickup buried his head under the feather pillow, as if he could banish the whole reality. Later, how much later he couldn't tell – the room was no lighter – there was a soft tapping on the door and Nicholson's whispered call. Later again

Nicholson was shaking him, commanding him to get up. Cold and hollow, Pickup forced himself into the world.

Thick yellowy vest, thick yellowy pants, thick grey flannels, splash at the washbasin, no need to shave – nor did Nick, nor probably Nicholson, only the black and adult Linné, whose Swiss clockwork machine was whirring in the next room – the comforting envelopment of the old grey polo neck sweater, socks, veldtschoen, sports coat, comb through the tangled wavy hair, the lavatory and nearly sick at its stale-meat German stink.

Down in the hotel lobby a pause while Linné spoke briefly with the porter. 'What about breakfast?' said Nick and Pickup would have echoed him but Nicholson shook his head sternly.

They deposited their luggage at the station, save Linné's little squat case – oh to be withdrawing it again! – and took a train that trundled south from the Karlsplatz into industrial streets hung with flags and posters. It was crammed with workers who sat or clung to the rails in silence, smoking. From the platform of the leading blue and white car Pickup watched the trailer car lurch and buck round the bends as if steered by an unseen driver who always left it too late... He felt Linné nudging him. They left the tram at the next stop, the morning air raw again after the smoke and potato smell of humanity.

The works presented a long institutional façade to the street, a line of heavy arched windows on each side of a massive main entrance above which the name Bayerische Beaton Linné stretched in letters of bronze. Linné led them in. From a cubicle by the door a uniformed porter began to accost them officiously, then recognised Linné, who raised his arm – and Pickup blinked, not ready for it – in the *Hitler-grüss* before warmly slapping the man on his back and making some ritual remark, perhaps in the local slang, which brought a chuckling reply.

They waited five minutes on a leather bench in a big echoing hall lit by the arched windows and hung with sombre portraits. Another porter, one empty sleeve tucked in his side pocket, led them stiffly down a corridor. An outer office all mahogany and frosted glass, then through the inner door and a worried-looking man peeling off the cloth cuff-protectors as he bowed and smiled and greeted Linné and, in turn, Nick and Nicholson and Pickup, warmly enough –

even ingratiatingly – but with some embarrassment, too, it seemed. He gestured, sighed, appealed to each of them for sympathy, shrugged, finally jumped up and went into another office farther down the corridor from where his muffled voice continued to sound intermittently.

Linné hissed, 'Watch out for me,' and slipped behind the desk, running his finger down the page of the desk diary that was open on it. The man had left the door open. Nicholson stealthily closed it until all but one corner of the inner office was masked from anyone passing in the corridor. He said, 'What's up?'

Linné said without looking up, 'Oh, that fool Ristow is being difficult. Says that petrol rationing has come in since we were last here, they have to account for every journey.' He finished with the note-tablet and slid open the deep drawer of a metal filing cabinet, fingering deftly through the suspended files. He glanced up a moment at Nicholson who mouthed 'Okay.'

Linné said, 'Here we are. Bavarian ministry of education– Damn, that's marvellous, isn't it, along with all the schools and the university and the Tech. – Dachau – Type E. 12 turbine, Type 800 generator, serviced monthly, see letter reference so-and-so, fuller service every third month, namely February, May, August and November – couldn't be better.' He pushed the drawer home and wandered coolly round the desk as Nicholson frowned a warning.

Ristow returned looking slightly less worried. Behind him was a stocky, upright man with a bristle of grey hair and hard eyes which stared at the visitors and then flicked suspiciously round the office in which they had been left alone, as if noting each exposed document and unlocked file. Pickup shrank from what he recognised instinctively as one of nature's sergeant-majors, but Linné was advancing as cool as you please, greeting the newcomer with extravagant bonhomie, again producing the *Hitlergrüss* before wringing his hand. Magically the hard eyes relaxed. In a moment they were all being introduced. Pickup didn't catch the name, only the title *Hauptmann* which he knew meant 'Captain.' Self-consciously he followed the others in giving the Hitler salute though without Nicholson's clicking of heels and snapping to attention. There was more conversation, laughter at a joke, then another round of elaborate handshakes and salutes before they were at last on their way.

'Nasty moment, that,' murmured Nick as the worried-looking man led them past a drawing office.

'Who was he?'

Linné muttered, 'The military supervisor, he's called. Appointed by the Münchener Büro. Supposed to guard the secrets of the works. Since all the patents are Swiss it's a bit pointless.'

'You handled him very well.'

'He's a fool, like all the others. A bit of flattery, called him Captain when I know for a fact he was never more than a lieutenant, dropped my father's name a few times. It was easy.'

They traversed a great store-room with rows of steel shelves reaching from floor to ceiling, went out through another door, and there it was in a yard beyond the stores, parked under a projecting asbestos roof with two others of the same kind. Pickup blinked. He'd been imagining something fairly solid and enclosed; this was a three-wheeler with the single wheel at the front and the driver's compartment largely taken up by what looked like the front half of a motor bike, the little box of a hold made of canvas over hoops.

Linné signed a paper, clambered into the driving seat and after jerking at a pull-up handle several times – to anxious advice from Nick and Nicholson as well as Ristow – started the motor which pop-pop-popped away explosively, producing much blue smoke and making the whole flimsy vehicle vibrate. Nicholson perched on the seat beside Linné while Nick and Pickup bent their heads and climbed through flapping canvas curtains into the back. There was just room for the two of them to sit down with their legs straight out. If they looked over their shoulders they could see through an aperture into the driving compartment. To a crescendo of popping and a series of jerks they moved slowly off. Clutching one of the iron hoops for support Pickup felt the van slow down again at the gate, then after an even jerkier start swing hard right into the street. Craning round Pickup saw that they were heading back towards the centre of the city. After the Horch the ride was painfully unsprung. The engine raced and faltered under Linné's inexpert control; once he stalled it altogether, another time Pickup was thrown against the side of the van as it was wrenched to one side. He winked at Nick who was grimacing in exaggerated consternation.

After about ten minutes they stopped as abruptly as they had started. Nicholson's face filled the aperture. 'Just changing drivers,' he said tersely.

'Not before time,' said Nick. 'We've been bounced about like billiard balls. What on earth were you doing, Phil?'

Linné said, 'You damn well try it yourself if you're–'

Nicholson's voice cut him off. 'It's a miracle we got this far. I thought we were going to be stopped once.'

Pickup said, 'What about that coffee?'

'Shouldn't we get on?'

Linné said, 'I told you, we don't want to get there too soon.'

Nick said, 'Where are we?' He unzipped Linné's case and drew out the Thermos flask. 'Dachauerstrasse.'

'Quiet?'

'Fairly.'

'Come on, let's. We need it.' He was already unscrewing the aluminium cap. He filled it and pushed it through the aperture.

Nicholson said a moment later, 'God, what did you put in it?'

'Deutscher brandy. Isn't it nice?'

'Excellent. But not too much of it, anyone.'

The cup came Pickup's way. The coffee was hot and sticky and heady. It filled him with an instant sense of wellbeing. Gradually they all relaxed a little. Linné said, 'Sorry about the driving but – two-stroke and a motor-bike clutch, it takes some getting used to.'

Nick said, in his more usual manner, 'I thought you were going to leave us behind a couple of times.'

Pickup felt a sudden, almost hysterical reversal of spirits, seeing Linné and Nicholson gravely motoring away on one wheel, he and Nick coasting after them on two.

'Another thing,' said Linné, 'the damned wheels fit the tramlines.'

'Get caught in them,' said Nicholson, sensing the change of mood, 'you're on your way to the depot.'

Pickup giggled out loud. Nick passed the cup to him again. He had a vague mental picture of the sweet, fumey liquor seeping into his veins, staining the blood as in the chemistry lab at school the permanganate or phenol had dripped lazily dissolving tendrils of colour into the beaker of clear solution under the burette.

They drove on more smoothly this time, the rear curtains flapping. It was just like

Nicholson, Pickup thought – though admiringly rather than enviously, in the warm aftermath of the coffee – to be instantly proficient at driving a two-stroke D.K.W. he'd never seen before. When they stopped again they were beyond the city. The damp, misty air held the lavatory smell of the cabbage fields that stretched on either side. Nicholson had drawn off under the shelter of a clump of trees. Heavy lorries with trailers – sometimes two – thundered past: otherwise there was little traffic. Linné pulled out two sets of crumpled blue overalls from his case. He and Nick took off their jackets and put on first the baggy trousers, then the short loose jacket buttoned up to the neck, lastly the floppy peaked cap. In the bald light of day they made unlikely-looking electricians. Nicholson frowned, pushed their caps out of shape, made Linné give up his spectacles, put his hand under the van and distributed some dirt.

'That's enough,' protested Linné. 'We are supposed to be a bit more than mechanics, you know. By the way, did you see that sign from inside there?'

'What sign?' said Pickup, fumbling in the case for the sketchbook and Pelikan drawing pen that was to be his equipment.

185

'Sign pointing the way to Dachau.'

'No. What about it?'

'Nothing.'

Nick said, 'Who drives now?'

Nicholson said, 'You have a go.'

Linné: 'Don't you think it would look more logical if the man who did the talking were also in charge of the van?'

'Not necessarily. It wouldn't look logical at all if he stalled the engine or ran over the commandant. Let's see how Nick manages.' He climbed into the truck with Pickup.

Nick managed well enough. Presently houses began to dot the side of the road. They overtook one of the lorry trains that had passed by. They bumped over a level crossing whose bell began to toll and long striped arms to descend as they cleared it. When they stopped for the third time Pickup, peering through the flaps, saw station buildings, a signal gantry looming behind, a yellow Post Office bus and an ancient taxi parked in front–

'Keep down,' hissed Linné.

'What's the matter?'

'There's something going on. Two policemen–'

'What sort?'

'Civil. But with them someone who looks

like one of the guards.'

'Rank?'

'Hard to say. Non-commissioned, I should think. Baggy uniform, big boots, soft hat, has a bicycle.'

'What are they doing?'

'The guard's doing all the talking and pointing. The police are listening.'

Nicholson said, 'We can't just sit here. Better drive on.'

'Where?'

'Anywhere.'

Nick said, 'But which direction? On or back the way–'

Linné's voice broke in again. 'Wait! The guard is going, I think. Yes, Heil Hitler. About turn–'

'Prepare to mount bicycles ... mount! Ooops.' Squinting through the aperture past Nick's head Pickup could just glimpse the ungainly figure. No one laughed but the tension slackened again.

Linné said, 'The police are going into the station. This might be the moment...'

'Anyone else about?'

'Can't see anyone. The guard's just rounding the corner... He's gone.'

'Right. You've given us a lift, remember.'

Nicholson led the way. Pickup followed

him clumsily, reaching for the sketch pad. Nick and Linné climbed out of the front compartment. Linné stamped his feet on the ground and stretched. He proposed a drink in loud, coarse German, mimicking the action of raising a glass to his lips. Nicholson and Pickup looked at each other, as planned, and shook their heads.

'So...' Linné stuck out his hand. They said noisy farewells all round, Nick and Linné adding a perfunctory salute before heading for the station *Gaststube*. Seeing them again in the crumpled blue overalls Pickup thought perhaps they didn't look so unlikely after all.

Nicholson and he walked away from the station along a street separated from the railway line by a strip of grassland; crossed a more important thoroughfare and then branched on to a narrow gravel road – more of a path than a road, really – which followed first a little stream and then the swirling, green-brown river into which the stream flowed. There were little houses of painted wood, neat and pretty as toys. Pickup wondered who lived in them and what they thought, if ever they thought, of what was done on the other side of Toytown.

Nicholson said, 'Are you sure this is the

right way?'

'Not the quickest but the most appropriate for an artist. We came this way that time in the summer.' Then the sun had been shining and the gravel had crunched drily underfoot; now it yielded soggily in a mist that was almost rain.

Nicholson looked at his watch and said, 'How much further?'

'We'll be there in plenty of time. We turn off when we come to a bridge.' That time before they'd kept on by the river, the path narrowing to a trail through the woods that teased them, hiding the water then revealing it again until it brought them to the bathing place.

At the bridge they left the river by a wider, but still empty, road. But muffled and flattened by the mist came the clang of shunted rail trucks, the rumble of a passing lorry, the lower unbroken hum of the Amper-und-Isar Werke. They came to an open triangular green two or three hundred yards across, framed by roads and bisected by a stream. On two sides it was bordered by half-timbered cottages and houses, unexceptional but pleasant enough, Pickup thought, to be sketched by an architectural student. On the third side, an iron fence, barriers, a wooden guard house, closed off a tree-lined avenue leading to a prospect of yellow buildings. In front of the gates stood a sentry.

Nicholson narrowed his eyes. 'Is that it?'

'Not it itself. Those are the barracks. You can just see the camp beyond.'

Pickup led the way across the grass to where there was a resting place with a pair of wooden benches and a stone carved to the memory of some ancient benefactor.

'Here?' said Nicholson.

'I thought so.'

'Not bad, not bad at all.' He sat down on the nearer bench with his back to the barrack entrance and lit a cigarette. Pickup perched on the end of the bench, opened the sketch pad and unscrewed the Pelikan. The memorial, beyond it the stream, beyond that roofs and trees unexpectedly sharpened by the mist, made an obvious picture, and from the corner of his eye he could see the sentry and the barrier lifting as he watched to let out a grey painted car—

Nicholson said, 'Can you see all right?'

'Well enough. Grey Opel just came out. You should see it in a second.'

'Good. Yes, I see it. That's the main road to the station?'

'Towards the station, yes.' He worked at the drawing. For a short while there was silence broken only by the squeak of the nib on the paper.

Nicholson said, 'They're about due. You're clear about everything?'

'Yes.'

Nicholson said, 'Here they come.' He might have been talking about a visiting rugger team.

Pickup forced himself to concentrate on the drawing, hatching in the shadow of the eaves of a distant house before looking up again. In the corner of his vision he saw the sentry, the guardhouse, the barrier – nothing more, nothing happening. He looked down, saw with surprise the pen was shaking in his hand, looked up again. Still nothing. Had he missed? – then all at once the little van was pulling up at the barrier. He heard Nicholson's voice behind him.

'Are they there?'

'Yes.'

'What's happening?'

'Nothing.'

'What do you mean nothing?'

They're just waiting there.' His eyes were watering. He screwed them shut for a moment and then risked turning his head more towards the scene. Nothing had changed. Without intent he scratched a line in the drawing. He heard Nicholson drop his cigarette end and stamp it out with his foot. Suddenly there was a noise.

'What was that?'

'Sounded like their horn.'

Almost immediately another, louder noise sounded, harsh blows of noise that seemed to bruise the air–

He looked wildly at Nicholson, 'That's the camp siren – something's gone wrong. What do we do?'

'Shut up. Keep your hair on and for God's sake keep your eye on that van. What's happened.'

'Still there in front of the barrier.'

'All right. It's probably some routine signal. They have them all day according to that character Philipp found in London.' After a second he went on, 'But to be on the safe side I'm going to wander away exactly two minutes from now if there's been no change. Thereafter, the plan as arranged. Don't look at me. Nod if you understand.'

Pickup nodded, but even as he did so he saw a uniformed figure leave the guard-house and approach the van. 'Hold on,' he hissed. 'Something's happening.'

The figure bent over, seemed to be peering inside the cab. Pickup held his breath. Then the little van began to move again but not ahead. It inched slowly round in a tight circle, the front wheel as hard over as it would go.

'They're turning round,' he told Nicholson. 'They're coming away again, they're coming away,' he was almost shouting with relief that welled up inside him. Unthinking he closed the sketch pad and started to get up–

'Stay where you are,' snapped Nicholson. 'Sit down.'

'All right,' he said more coolly a little later. 'They've gone by. But we'll give them a few minutes more.'

Pickup looked absently at his drawing. It needed a bit of movement, he decided, and inked in a little figure. He glanced sideways at the barrack entrance and stiffened. 'Ian! Something's happening.' As he watched he saw the barriers lift, and presently through the gap came a fantastic, shambling army.

The green frock coat someone had identified as that of the Prussian civil police at the turn of the century, the grey jersey as the stable jersey worn by the cavalry. The ancient white trousers defied recognition. The dress uniform of a Dachauer! Creased and musty from the stores it had been issued to them. With many a coarse joke from the orderlies. For Klaus Ihde, each grotesque garment had meant earnest deliberation; shall I put them on, these strange stiff trousers, or shall I cast myself at an end? He had one foot in the trousers, trying to force a decision. Run from the building across the square, one last assertion of the failing Ihde ego, and naked receive the bullets unslowed even by the thickness of cloth? Holding one heavy boot in his hand the proposition had been to assail a guard and perhaps give him a broken cheekbone before dying. But each time he had been held back – by what?

Not hope any more. The last faint spark, fanned to brightness by the rumours of release, had burned out when he learned it was not freedom he was marked for but transfer. The officer who had briefly addressed them on the square had been less hectoring than usual, had almost tried to reassure them. Where they were going Jews and Aryans were in separate camps. As Aryans they would have proper conditions. For the Jews – he had paused and twisted his face – for the Jews only What the pigs deserved. The destination, when he named it, could still dismay even a Dachauer. Buchenwald! In the bragging talk of the 'Greens,' the old criminals who knew only prisons and prison lore, Buchenwald was claimed to make Dachau appear a sanatorium.

For Klaus, where he was going mattered little by the side of the time of his going. On the very morning of the desperate venture proposed for him from outside. Was it a theatrical attempt by God to force him to believe? – if misery had failed, try irony? But as they marched through the S.S. barracks, each scarecrow figure clutching under his arm a paper parcel of the few possessions he was allowed to keep, Klaus summoned a remaining flicker of honesty. He couldn't deny he hadn't felt a pulse of relief. He was one who shrank from deeds. He hadn't run naked against the wire, he hadn't sprung on the guard. Would he have been able to propel himself into that other undertaking? It wasn't the danger, the prospect of death, that he feared but having to make the decision to ACT. The Bible-boy Emil might have spurred him to it but the Bible-boy Emil, when he had muttered the secret to him down by the rubble-hill in the far corner of the camp, had trembled in consternation, mumbling that he dared not ... he would be fleeing God as well as fleeing man. At the same time the child was plainly liquefied with fear in expectation of those forty lashes. It could have been that the flesh would have propelled *him* whatever the price...

They were leaving the barracks now, the guards at either side of the motley green and white column bracing themselves even more fiercely upright, shouting and snapping their orders. It must have been a hastily-organised transport; they preferred to receive and despatch their parties at the sidings within the S.S. enclave. To march the three kilometres to the town station was a bonus. He stared hungrily at the world he had not seen for a year: houses of slack civilian outline and dipping roofs; an ox cart; a dog barking; a woman with a shopping basket, black stockings, probably quite old; children on the green; and a young man – no, two young men – who stared for a minute then turned and strode away.

There would be shops nearer the town centre, perhaps a private motor-car, a cinema poster; then the train, a glimpse of Munich from the windows, bridges, rivers, people, the woods and slopes of Franconia, and finally Weimar – Goethe's Weimar, O

Goethe, come to what? And when he had seen all that could be seen and the gates had closed behind them and the wire bounded them again and there was nothing more to see – then he would do it. This time he would do it, quickly, before the habit of survival could take hold again.

Nick said, 'How long did we sit there? It seemed like a week.'

'Four minutes exactly,' said Nicholson.

Nick laughed his braying laugh. 'Thought we were done for. The fellow – he looked like a gorilla – just looked at us and picked up the telephone. Kept looking at us as he talked.'

Linné said, 'Then you blew the damned horn.'

'I didn't mean to. God, no. I had my finger on the button and suddenly the bloody thing sounded. I thought the gorilla was going to have apoplexy.'

'I smiled my sickly smile,' said Linné.

'His face went filthy and he shouted some-thing–'

'To wait.'

'–and went back to the phone.'

'Then *their* siren went–'

'We heard it.'

'–I thought it was all up.'

'Then, of course,' said Linné, 'we saw this column shambling down the road towards us, and this fellow came back out of the guardhouse – he was about seven feet high, when he put his hand on the van it rocked – and bawled into the cab–'

'That the camp was closed, we'd have to come back later...'

The braying laugh again, as if he found the homely phrase funny.

'Because of these people?' said Nicholson, ignoring the joke.

'He didn't go into details,' said Linné. 'He just said *raus!* but I suppose so, yes.'

'How many were there?'

'You saw them better than us.'

'Two hundred, anyway.' Nicholson frowned. 'I wonder what's up.'

They were parked in the quiet road from the river. The relief, for the moment, was total. Deliberately, almost gratefully Pickup let himself worry about what once more seemed the more pressing reality: his absence, now in its third day, from classes. Wednesday morning, it should be Heat Engines with the impenetrable Jolliffe. He said, 'Well, we tried. We weren't to know they were going to start graduating today.'

'No one could have foreseen it,' said Linné.

Nicholson said, 'Do you suppose Helmuth's friend was one of them?'

Linné shrugged.

Pickup said, 'Well, oughtn't we to be thinking of getting back?'

'Getting back where?'

'To Munich, of course. The train goes at twelve, remember.'

Nicholson looked at him in that bleak way of his. 'But it's only nine-thirty. And we haven't done what we came to do. Didn't you hear what Nick said? We're to go back later.'

'But I thought ... I mean, isn't it tempting fate a bit?"

'Tempting fate,' echoed Nicholson in a mincing voice, and lengthening the 'a' in a crude imitation of the accent which Pickup would put on when in the mood, which Nicholson himself had often enough encouraged. 'I'd hardly call it that. Would you, Nick? Phil?'

Nick, uncomfortable, said nothing. Linné looked at his hands. 'Well, not exactly–'

'I assumed that we were agreed on going through with this. Of course, Mickup, if you want to withdraw at this stage I'm sure we can manage without you.'

'I don't. It's just that ... well...'

Nicholson said, 'Turn your head.'

'What...?'

'You see. I always said that receding chin was a bad sign–'

Pickup lashed out with his foot. Nicholson moved aside and his shoe hit the side of the van.

'Temper,' said Nicholson. 'I think perhaps we *should* do without you. After all, yours isn't a very perilous task.'

Pickup, shamed but still hating him, said, 'You can talk! Who's going to be safely on his way back to the Consulate if the balloon goes up?'

'Take that back!'

'You take back–'

'Take it back!' His face was rigid.

'Oh for heaven's sake stop it, you two,' said Linné.

'I'm not taking that from an ill-bred weed!'

'Shut up,' said Nick, 'or we'll all be inside for a breach of the peace or something.'

There was a silence.

'I was going to propose,' said Nicholson, 'that I should change places with Nick. Philipp's German makes him indispensable,

I'm afraid.'

Linné nodded mutely as if only too conscious of the fact. The thought struck him. 'But they've already seen Nick in the van – perhaps remember him.'

'You could have changed your mate during the morning.'

Nick, looking down at his hands, said, 'No, I'll go again.' Stinging still from his own humiliation Pickup dully sensed his fear.

## CHAPTER 8

The Pelikan nib dug into the paper softened and swollen by the thin drizzle that was now falling. Pickup scribbled blindly, uncaringly, at what must have been the twentieth drawing he had made. The second vigil was infinitely worse than the first. The little van had driven up to the entrance and been admitted almost immediately, the fearful siren sounding from beyond the barracks as the barrier closed behind it. Nicholson had waited silently behind him until with a terse farewell he had departed for the station. By now he would be on his way to Munich while Pickup sketched on unnaturally in the rain. He felt that eyes, lenses must be turned upon him. Once a lorry had rumbled out of the camp, down the road behind him and instead of going on had turned along the third side of the triangle on his right ... coming for him, he felt so sure, that a kind of cold dispassion replaced his first feelings of panic. But the lorry had gone on, passing him not ten yards away.

Now the sentry, every time he risked an oblique glance in that direction, seemed to be staring fixedly at him. How long had they been inside? Willing himself not to look at his watch just yet he sought refuge in thinking about that other time he'd been here, the day he'd subsequently, secretly edged in red ink in his diary. They'd parked the car near the Schloss and walked, taking the gravelled path that led to the river. Jill was wearing pleated shorts – a few heads turned disapprovingly in the street – and her legs were brown and slim. She walked between Nick and Pickup, unpredictably friendly and gay, even took both their arms. Pickup had blinked a little prayer of thanks that Helmuth should have had a flying thing to do – to think he'd asked Pickup if he'd like to go with him and he'd nearly accepted! – while Nicholson and Linné were going out to some boring BBL site.

It had been very hot and still. The Amper was dark and smooth, with darker depths to it. They went past a swimming place which had some changing huts and was full of children, and along the bank beyond where there was no path and the trees pressed almost to the water's edge. But they'd found a sunny clearing and settled themselves for their picnic and swim and unrolling his towel Pickup had found to his dismay that he hadn't brought his trunks. Nick had laughed and said to wear his underpants, but he knew they were much too flappy and gapey and when they were wet they would have shown everything and looked awful, too, and THEN Jill had said why didn't they all go in without, the Germans did. Without more ado she'd skipped away unfastening things and slithering out of them and suddenly, he couldn't believe it, was advancing into the river absolutely bare, grinning back at them over one freckled shoulder, her bottom very white and when she half turned, the light just catching the fuzz of hair he'd always thought would be so ugly but now wasn't – then Nick, too, braying as if it was just a joke and not something beautiful. And quickly, without letting himself think, wishing only that he had more muscle and that men were neater to look at, Pickup had followed suit. It was so nice and natural that when he happened to look down a minute or two later and saw his private parts floating pallidly in the brown water it was quite a little shock.

Afterwards the Amerings put on their dry costumes and Pickup hitched his towel round his middle and they ate their picnic. Pickup basked in the sun and a haze of happiness and incredulity, not caring that Jill shared sandwiches and beer with her brother rather than with him, just as their jokes and clipped, monosyllabic conversation so often seemed to exclude the outsider. He'd never noticed such closeness between other brothers and sisters he knew. It was odd to think of them seeing each other, as they just had. Perhaps they'd grown up seeing each other all along ... then Jill was teasing Nick about his girl-friend and he was lying on his back and denying it and she suddenly leaned across and pinched the bulge in his swimming trunks and wriggled away laughing as he flailed at her—

He became aware of three little children, two boys and a girl shapeless in thick woollen stockings – even the boys – straying towards him across the wet grass with curious eyes, giggles, whispers. What did they want? To see what he was drawing? He looked down in dismay at the meaningless blots. The little girl was pretty even in her shapeless clothes and boots. The thought struck him, she was from the barracks? He remembered something the gaunt man had told them, about when the wind was from the West the prisoners would hear the children's voices– Oh hell, he had to get away from this place. The despair must have shown on his face for the children backed away, eyes wide, only giggling shrilly again as they turned and ran.

He glanced nervously to see if the sentry had been watching and saw – for an instant without belief, not daring to believe, then with a great tremor of hope – the little van at the barrier, already there, stationary. O please God make it lift and everything come all right. It wasn't going to lift, they were caught – it lifted! Pickup's last strand of restraint snapped. Instead of waiting a minute or two before sauntering away he broke into a lumbering trot, intent only on getting aboard, getting away with the others, being alone no longer.

The van had turned off again along the lonely leafy road that led to the river. Pickup laboured after it, panting, oblivious of appearances until he saw it was slowing down and in a sudden access of guilt realised what he was doing and pressed himself, panting, against a wire fence to look back and see if he were followed.

It was all right. As he ran to the van again it began to move off. Panicking he pulled himself into the back, banging his knee. He panted through the aperture. 'Done?' Linné half turned his head and nodded. Pickup mouthed 'Super' but Linné made no acknowledgement. If he were exultant he didn't show it. He looked pale and his mouth was shut very tightly.

Once outside the town they stopped again for Nick and Linné to remove their overalls. Nick was also subdued, for him.

'What's the matter?' asked Pickup.

'Never mind that now,' said Linné. He rolled his overalls into a bundle and dropped them into the ditch.

'God, inside there,' said Nick. There was one fellow–' His voice broke off as it did when he was going to laugh, but he didn't laugh this time.

'For Christ's sake, we've a train to catch.'

'Not till twelve,' said Nick. He was rummaging in his folded jacket instead of putting it on again. He pulled out a flat glass bottle and unscrewed the cap.

Linné swore again. 'Oh, leave that now. Don't forget we have to return the van – or I have to, even if you don't.'

'I need a drink.' He tipped his head back and sucked hungrily at the bottle.

'Come on,' urged Linné.

His tension re-infected Pickup. 'Yes, Nick, we ought to get going–'

'*Shut up.*' Nick had never spoken to him like that. 'You should have seen this fellow tied to a tree–'

'Leave that till later,' said Linné. 'What have you got there?' He grabbed the flask and sniffed. '*Brandy!* What would they think if we got stopped.'

'No one'll stop us.' He snatched it back

Linné started to get in behind the wheel. He said. 'Well, I'm going whether–'

The Dachau siren quivered in the air, distant but unmistakable. Nick jerked to action, scrambling after Linné and pushing him from the controls. Pickup climbing into the back, was flung off balance as the little motor raced and the van shot forward. The gears grated, a big diesel lorry coming up behind hooted reproachfully, then they were drawing away again. Pickup, clutching the iron hoops, watched the shiny wet road retreat. 'Come on! Faster, faster...'

Nick was driving like a Jehu. The little three-wheeler skidded and swayed, some loose tools in the back hammered on the floorboards with the vibration. The rear curtains flapped and cracked. For the hundredth time he looked at the watch strapped to the bony wrist by his head. Still an hour and forty minutes to the train. Nicholson would be at the hotel by now, waiting for them to return or telephone him. Though he had accused Nicholson of giving himself a soft job Pickup now thought guiltily that in fact it would be pretty nerve-racking. The hotel wasn't ideal, especially as they had booked out, really, but it wouldn't have done to involve Helmuth so directly and the Schottenhammel did happen to be mid-way between the station and the consulate. He saw Nicholson sitting on one of the brown leather seats in the hall place, pretending to read the paper, watching the porter for the nod to go into the little telephone cubicle. But it would be very busy today, with the city filling–

He was swung sideways suddenly, losing

his grip with one hand and lurching against the canvas side. He heard the brakes shuddering. He knew with utter clarity that they were skidding, even noted the road and trees and a telegraph pole whizzing diagonally past the gap in the rear curtains as instinctively he ducked his head and covered it in his hands. There were some dull bumps and finally a terrific bang. He felt a clout behind his right ear, his weight all on to his shoulders, his feet being thrust over his head as in a backward roll. He thought, we're turning over, then suddenly everything was still for an instant. He opened his eyes and his feet were above him, but tipping away again as he fell backwards and sideways and landed half kneeling, half on his side with his face pressed hard against the canvas. He said 'Hey' and scrambled out of the van on his hands and knees, surprised to find it meant going up hill. His legs felt funny so he kept hold of the back hoop. Linné was straightening up on his feet, about three yards away. One side of his face was streaked green and brown. He held one arm and looked back the way they'd come. Pickup followed his gaze. The edge of the road was level with his eyes. They'd broken through a wooden rail and come right off the road down a slope into a field.

Pickup said, 'That's torn it.'

Linné turned his head. He looked astonished. He said, 'I think I'll have to sit down,' which he did, flop, on the spot he occupied.

'Are you all right?'

'I think so. Where's Nick?'

Linné looked towards the van. 'I think he's– Oh, hell, the windscreen–'

Pickup called 'Nick.' Still holding on the hood he slithered round the other side of the van. He stopped, not daring to go on. He said 'Nick' again, in a lower voice, half-dreading a reply. Nick was on his knees, crouching, in a ball, one hand over his face, the other hugged to his middle. Pickup said, 'Nick, what's the matter?' He didn't want to look.

'*My eyes.*' A sort of whisper.

'Are you sure?' He bent over the huddled figure. 'I can't see. Can you look up.'

'I'd better not.' He said it quite conversationally, as if declining a cigarette.

Pickup knelt down and looked. There was blood everywhere, oozing through Nick's fingers. In his hair, dripping off his cuff, great blotches of it on the grass underneath him. He said, 'Move your hand, can you?' He glimpsed a kind of red triangular flap, something shiny white showing through the red. He smelled brandy. He looked away again quickly. 'I think it's only blood in them. You cut yourself but it's away from the eyes.'

He took his arm, the one he was hugging, meaning to say, 'Can you get up?' Before he could Nick screamed, 'Leave it.'

Pickup looked helplessly at Linné. The sight of him sitting on his bottom suddenly angered him. He shouted, 'For bloody hell's sake come and help.'

Linné said, 'Is it bad?'

'He's cut his head and one wrist.'

'What about the train?'

'I don't know.' He didn't, either. He could think of nothing. The whole situation seemed glassy and unreal. In a moment someone would press the switch again and they'd be back in the van, speeding along the Munich road.

Nick said in his conversational voice again, 'Have you got a handkerchief?'

Pickup said, 'It's not very clean.' He put it between the fingers of the hand clutched to the head. The finger shuffled it into place. Without moving his arms Nick drew one leg into a kneeling position and started to push himself up. Pickup got an arm round his waist and gestured to Linné to help the other side. Slowly they led Nick up to the road, actually getting behind and pushing him the last steep part.

The road was empty in either direction. There were houses a quarter of a mile away but nothing nearer. They sat Nick on the wooden rail, painted with red and white stripes that had marked the curve in the road he hadn't managed. The handkerchief was soaked already and blood covered his jacket and shirt and tie. Where he pressed his clenched hand to his middle there was a solid dark patch.

Pickup said, 'We'll have to get him to hospital.'

Nick said, 'Cigarette.' His voice was faint. What could be seen of his face through all the blood was deathly white and sweaty. He was trembling.

Pickup lit a Players and inserted it in his mouth and looked up the road again.

'Catch him!'

Just in time he grabbed Nick as he started to fall backwards off the rail. Linné helped lower him to the ground. Pickup found himself wriggling out of his jacket to make a pillow, as he'd often read in books. The cigarette was still stuck to Nick's lips, stained with blood that had trickled down the side of his nose. Pickup threw it away.

Linné said, 'There's something coming.'

It was a lorry or even–

Linné said, 'It's a *bus*.' He sounded as if he could cry.

'Then we'll catch it.'

He stepped into the road with arms outstretched, watching the bus approach. He knew somehow that it would stop. The long bonnet jutted in front like a nose. He could see the driver frowning through the windscreen. He must have seen Nick for as soon as he'd pulled up he opened the door and came clattering down the step carrying a tin box with a red cross on it. Pickup heard Linné answering his gruff challenge. He felt the stares of the bus passengers but for a moment didn't care. The driver had a first aid box, probably even knew about first aid; it would be all right, he'd stop the bleeding. He shut his eyes for a moment, listening to the slow *brrrm-brrm* of the idling diesel. When he looked up there was a pad of lint covering half Nick's face and the driver was starting to wind a bandage round it. Next the arm: Pickup flinched as the driver grunting and humming to himself, pulled out a big pocket knife with a horn handle but he only used it to slit Nick's sodden sleeve to the elbow. He peered at the bloody mess on his arm, clapped another lint on and tied it with a bandage above the wound.

Between them they lifted Nick awkwardly up the step and into the bus. The driver kept grunting little directions in German at them and over his shoulder to the other passengers, evidently telling them to keep back and not get in the way. There was a space at the front, just by the door, where there was only a tip-up seat which the driver pushed up out of the way. They laid Nick down, with his head on Pickup's jacket again, under the dashboard with his feet reaching into the central gangway. He looked terrible.

Linné took a vacant seat behind the driver, Pickup hesitated. There wasn't another seat near the front and now he didn't want to have to push down the bus past those staring faces and chattering tongues – then a boy in some elaborate boy scout uniform with tassels spraying from the shoulder was getting to his feet and waving Pickup to his place, next to a stout Frau who was squeezing over and smiling welcomingly. He mumbled a *Danke schön* and took the seat.

The bus moved off. Pickup tried to compose himself for whatever came next. He could see the driver's eyes reflected in the mirror above his head. They were narrowed in concentration, as if he were driving more quickly than usual. His uniform jacket had shoulder straps with piping and even a little star like an army officer's pips but his peaked hat was soft and saggy and grease-darkened round the edges like any bus-driver's at home, which was comforting. He changed gear with an enormous gear lever, it must have been four feet long. In the next village he slowed down for the bus-stop and a man in a green forester's jacket with oak leaves on the collar got on, stepping over Nick without excessive surprise and handing his money to the driver, who absent-mindedly, took it while shouting a question to another man he seemed to know who'd come out of a little shop nearby and who shook his head in reply and pointed towards Munich. Voices from the rear of the bus joined in debate. The driver swung the lever by his side that closed the door and pulled out into the road again. The trafficator was a big yellow arm which waved lazily up and down...

He became aware of the woman by his side saying something. He smiled vaguely at her and muttered. 'Sorry, we're English.'

The woman kept looking at Nick and clucking with concern, then looking back at him with exaggerated sympathy. She started to rummage in her basket. From the other side of the gangway came the unbroken stare of an old man whose face was bristly with white stubble, who smoked a long pipe which hung right down on to his chest and had a metal lid to the bowl–

He felt a nudge from the woman. At first he couldn't see what she wanted him to do, until he saw the packet of German cigarettes she was offering. He shook his head. She insisted. He tried to take one but the packet, though only of thin paper, open at the top, was too tightly packed. She shook her head again, pushing the whole packet into his hand. Touched, he tried to thank her, and finally succeeded in prising a cigarette out. It was strong and coarse-flavoured, unlike any cigarette he'd ever tasted before. He had to make an effort not to cough. After a bit it went out of its own accord.

The outskirts of the city began to absorb them. The bus drove on and now the driver was passing by people waiting at stops, waving his hand in front of him in a gesture to imply he couldn't help it. He pulled up only to let off a man and a woman who'd advanced from the rear of the bus. As they climbed down the man gave further directions, pointing on and then twisting his hand and jabbing it to indicate a right turn. At last the driver, screwing up his eyes again and looking for the turning, braked and swung the bus off the Dachauer-strasse through quieter side streets and there was a red cross road sign and a moment later they were stopping by iron gates and beyond, a little courtyard.

The driver hauled back a handbrake as massive as the gearlever and sprang down from the bus. Pickup saw him reach for an old-fashioned bell pull just inside the gates and heard the bell sounding faintly somewhere within the building. Linné followed, Pickup last. They stood awkwardly for a moment, until a nun appeared. She was young, with a round, smooth, colourless face and glasses. She looked with astonishment from the coatless Pickup to the mud-and-grass streaked Linné and finally into the bus at Nick. The driver jerked his arm in the direction from which they'd come as he explained. The nun bobbed her head and went back inside.

Pickup was suddenly cold. He felt himself shivering and wished for his tweed sports jacket. He was also very thirsty. He leaned against the bus mudguard, feeling the heat of the engine in his body, vaguely aware of another nun, a big strong nun in white instead of brown, and voices, and a man in overalls with a stretcher. He saw Nick being wheeled away and Linné following, then the nun, you could see her black boots beneath the long brown and white garments. He retrieved his jacket and was about to go after them when he felt a hand on his arm. The driver was fumbling with a pocket book, stiff brown covers enclosing loose buff forms. Pickup half understood, half guessed him to be saying something about names. On to the back of a form he printed their names, N. O. P. AMERING, P. LINNÉ, M. J. PICKUP, and C/O BRITISH CONSUL-GENERAL, MÜNCHEN. The driver seemed satisfied and turned to go. On the impulse Pickup held out his hand. They shook. The driver looked at Pickup as if looking at him for the first time, said *Ja, Ja* and a loud *Auf wiedersehen* and swung himself aboard. The stout woman was craning her head to look out. She caught Pickup's eye and gave him a warm, motherly smile.

Inside the hospital he was plunged into an atmosphere he recognised at once, from war stories, as the cloying heaviness of chloroform or alternatively iodoform. The walls were a sort of apricot colour, on them a crucifix complete with realistic hanging Jesus, sombre oil paintings of other religious subjects, an old notice printed in Gothic lettering, a newer one in slanting, inked Roman capitals. The floor was of ripply, slippery tiles.

Linné confronted him. 'What time do you make it? My damned watch stopped.'

Pickup looked. 'Twenty past. We must ring Ian.'

'Never mind Ian. What about the train?'

'We can't catch it now.'

'Why not? This is not so far away. I think I recognise where we are.'

'But we can't leave Nick.'

'He will be O.K. They are putting stitches in.'

'But we can't *leave* him – you know, all alone for when they find out.'

'We don't know that they will find out. Anyway what is the point in us all running that risk? What is achieved?'

Pickup groped for an answer.

'If we get away we can do something for him,' Linné said. 'Raise a great stink. Here, we'll all be in the soup together.'

There was sense in that, but–

'Anyway, it was his own stupid fault, driving so badly.'

That was mean, the sort of thing he said himself if he wasn't careful–

Linné said urgently, softly, 'Listen, Michael, you didn't go into that place. You didn't see what sort of beasts we're up against.'

'If we waited, couldn't we all get the next train?'

'There isn't a next train, not that's going to get us out of this country before tomorrow morning. Besides, if they start checking up on the van we may not have until tomorrow morning.'

'Will they?'

'Sooner or later, of course.'

Pickup thought guiltily of the names he'd just written down for the bus driver. He stared at Linné in an agony of indecision. Linné stared back. For the first time Pickup saw him as someone of his own age. The mask of assurance had gone. He was insecure and frightened like anyone else, even silly-looking with his face streaked green and ochre–

*'Come on!'*

Pickup started to move, then remembered

something. 'Hey! What about Ian?'

'We can telephone him from the station.'

'But that will be too late – he'll have left the hotel.'

'Then we get him at the Consulate.'

'He'd never go without Nick.'

'That's his affair.'

Pickup shook his head in dismay. 'We can't,' he wailed. 'We *can't.*'

Somewhere in the building a bell had started to toll, light and clear in tone. Nearer, there was the tip-tap of footsteps on the shiny tiles.

Linné said, 'You fool, Michael, you stupid fool.'

The nun came up to them, the first one, the young round-faced one. She smiled and motioned them to follow her along the corridor. The bell stopped. There was a cabbagy cooking smell. The nun led them into an office with another crucifix on the wall, a huge cupboard with labels pasted on the doors, a roll-top bureau and on it – a telephone. The nun dipped a pen in ink and began to ask questions. Pickup nudged Linné, pointing to the phone. The nun smiled assent. There was a long wait getting through to the hotel. Linné cupped his hand over the mouthpiece and resumed spelling out A-M-E-R-I-N-G. Pickup thought, it's too late, he'll have gone to the Consulate; well, perhaps that was for the best – then Linné was asking for Herr Nicholson and straightaway, it seemed, switching to English to tell him what had happened.

Pickup could hear the quack of consternation from the other end. Linné whispered into the phone as if to prevent anyone else hearing. After a couple more exchanges he looked up and asked for the name of the hospital and the address.

'What's happening?' hissed Pickup as the nun took the handset and carefully replaced it.

'He said to wait here. He's coming out.'

Pickup nodded.

'And, Michael–'

'Yes?'

'No need to tell him what we were just discussing, eh?'

In another hospital in another city Ernst vom Rath, third secretary at the German embassy in Paris, was dying from the five bullets fired into his body forty-eight hours before by Herschel Grunspan, the son of a Jewish tailor who had lately been deported from Hanover to the Polish frontier. He lay on a high wheeled bed without a pillow; suspended above it was a bottle from which blood dripped down a tube into his arm. His face had the colour and sheen of the wax used in candles in church.

Nicholson regarded them accusingly, as if it had been all their fault, Pickup's especially. He'd changed his shirt since the morning, donned his Wellington tie, polished his shoes and retrieved his trench coat. His hair was brushed flat. His face shone pinkly. He said, 'Did you have to let him drive?'

'You hardly encouraged my driving.'

'And Mickup?'

'I don't–'

'Of course, Mickup doesn't drive.'

They were in a little square room dis-tempered the same shiny apricot colour, hung with the same religious objects. There were two beds; one was empty, on the other lay Nick, covered with a thick blue rug. His head and one arm and hand were freshly bandaged. He was asleep, breathing quite deeply now.

Nicholson asked, 'They didn't say when he could go?'

'They didn't say anything about going.'

'How long does that stuff take to wear off?'

No one knew.

'You saw the doctor?'

Linné said, 'We told you. Only for a minute.'

'Was he inquisitive?'

'He wanted to know what had happened.'

'Do they have to tell the police?'

'In this country nothing happens that isn't told either to the local party snoop or the police. But here we may be lucky...'

Pickup said, 'It's not a proper hospital you know. Just a little place he runs himself, pretty well, mostly for women, I think.'

Nicholson said, 'I started looking up the timetables in the hotel when I didn't hear from you. The train tonight doesn't cross the border until seven in the morning. That's leaving it late if...' He shrugged. 'Well, if they close the frontiers. And at this rate there's no guarantee we can even catch that.'

Linné said, 'But there must be other trains out of the Reich. To Paris, or for that matter to—'

'I thought of that already. Not to mention jolly old Lufthansa.'

'*Fly*, you mean?' Pickup felt a bump of excitement: to be whirled away magically; and the thrill of the flight on top. A Ju 52 trimotor, or maybe even one of the sleek new Ju 86s.

'There is the small difficulty of money,' Nicholson added. 'How much has everyone got?'

Pickup had fifteen marks; Nicholson fifty, Linné the most with 120. Nick's wallet, deposited on a bedside table with other possessions, yielded only another thirty. 'He spent about a hundred on some bangle for Jill,' said Nicholson without expression.

Linné said, 'The nearest country is Switzerland.'

'I was thinking that. How long does it take by train?'

Through Bregenz three or four hours, I should think, depending on the connection.'

'Mmm.' Nicholson deliberated briefly before going on. 'I was also thinking that one of us should get away now, to pull strings if necessary.'

Linné's and Pickup's eyes met.

Pickup said, 'Who?'

'Not you, Mickup. Nor me, in case that's what you're thinking. Philipp's the man.'

'No, no, I couldn't,' protested Linné.'

'Just listen: you're at home in Switzerland, your father lives there, he's powerful, he has a lot of influence with the German government. Besides, you have the most to lose.'

'How is that?'

Nicholson sat on the unoccupied bed. 'Being a German yourself, or so they'd say ... that sort of thing.'

Pickup said, 'Yes, you go, Phil.'

Linné said nothing.

Nicholson said, 'I take it that's settled, then.'

Linné said casually, 'There's a train about four as far as I remember.'

'You've plenty of time, then. What time would you be at your father's?'

'With luck by ten o'clock.'

'Just when the...'

Linné nodded.

'Give us the telephone number. What are the Huns like on foreign phone calls?'

'They listen in, I imagine, but they usually put you through.'

'If we don't get away at all today we'll try and speak to you around midnight. If we're on the way we may not be able to, of course.'

'And if I don't hear from you?'

'Start breaking it to Papa gently. Square the van with him at least. If you've still not heard by breakfast time, give him the works.'

They walked with Linné out of the little

hospital and through the streets to the tram stop. It was the end of the line, and the two linked blue and white cars were waiting as they turned the corner. Linné broke into a run and the others followed him, but it was another five minutes before the driver clambered on to the front platform ready to move off. They talked desultorily. For the moment Pickup was worrying only about the thirst which had persisted all morning and grown worse after the bowl of salty noodle soup and hunk of dry bread the young nun had brought for them.

Linné gave them fifty Reichsmarks and all the English money he had, keeping the rest for his journey. They didn't shake hands but Linné waved until the tram rattled round the corner and was gone. Pickup felt numb and vaguely – but not specifically – depressed. He licked his dry lips and said, 'I don't suppose we could get a beer, could we?'

Nicholson said unexpectedly, 'Why not? Good idea.'

Emerging at last from the half-litre glass Pickup belched to himself and dimly considered the familiar exhortatory posters of square-chinned bare-torsoed Aryan men and cog-wheels and sheaves of wheat which together with a handwritten football bill were pinned on the wall of the little *gaststube*.

Nicholson said, 'I never asked how they got on.'

'In the camp, you mean? They did it.'

'No trouble?'

'Apparently not. There was this guard who took them to the turbine house. Looked as if he were going to stay with them, which was jolly awkward. Nick daren't open his mouth. But after a bit he asked Phil how long they'd be and locked them in and went away.'

'And the thing is set to go?'

'Yes. At ten o'clock tonight.'

Nicholson hesitated. 'Did they say what it was like inside?'

Pickup finished his beer. 'They both looked shaken. Phil didn't say anything except when – except that we couldn't know if we hadn't been in. Nick was the one who showed more, funnily. He kept going on about someone tied to a tree.'

'How tied to a tree?'

'I don't know,' said Pickup. 'With his arms tied behind it, I think. Sort of hanging.' Even here, six on seven miles away, it seemed unreal, impossible. He said, 'It's weird, isn't it? The people on the bus – they stared and

228

stared but they were kind. They wanted to help. The driver was super. And in that little hospital, the nuns – well, they're nice in their way. Even the old boy that brought out a stretcher for Nick was ... gentle.' To his dismay he felt his eyes prickling again. Hastily he changed the subject.

'It must have taken a lot of guts.'

'What?'

'Going into the place like that – Nick and Phil.'

Nicholson considered the matter. He said, 'It sounds as if Nick rather went to pieces. Philipp, yes, he was admirable – until he ran out of indignation.'

'I don't see...'

'Why else do you think I–' He broke off. Then: 'Look, Mickup, if this kind of thing is going to be done at all it's going to be done by men who enjoy doing it and are good at doing it – not by men with axes to grind.'

In the hospital in Paris it was all over. The stillness of the wax face had subtly altered, become permanent. The blood drip had been disconnected. An embassy official who had been waiting in an ante-room stood up, shook hands with the assistant secretary from the foreign ministry and the detective who had shared his vigil and left for the embassy in the Rue de Lille.

The doctor had watery blue eyes and strands of thin brown hair arranged across his head. In the morning he'd been wearing a white smock fastened at the back, with a white surgical mask hanging round his neck. Now he was just in an ordinary crumpled double-breasted suit. He was comically disconcerted by the loss of the German speaker from the party.

'He had to go to his father,' said Nicholson slowly, and loudly. 'His father – vater — sehr krank, muss zu hause schnell gehen.'

'Tell him we've got to go, too,' urged Pickup.

'Shut up.'

The doctor stared distractedly at the crucifix as if seeking help from that quarter. He said, 'Ihre friend ... she must not...' He switched to German, rapid and almost inaudible, a gesture to himself rather than to them. His shoes squeaking loudly, he led them down the tiled corridor to Nick's room. Nick had come round an hour earlier, been a little sick and taken some peppermint tea from a porcelain thing like a little teapot. He was dozing again but opened the one eye that showed from beneath his bandages. The doctor felt his pulse and addressed him quietly in German.

'What's he want?' asked Nicholson.

There was a lag before Nick replied, in not much more than a whisper. 'He wants to know where you'd take me. He says I mustn't travel yet.'

'Tell him the vons and zus,'

'But–'

'Tell him. It'll be all right.'

The doctor turned to Nicholson for confirmation. Nicholson nodded vigorously and repeated the vons and zus name, and gave their address.

'And she can … rest there?'

'Bestimmt.'

The doctor pondered. He led them back into the corridor. He frowned, hunting for the words to state his decision now he had made it. 'She must rest for two, three days.'

They signified understanding and agreement. 'We hope you will visit him each day,' Nicholson added.

The doctor seemed to get that. He smiled a bit unbelievingly, Pickup thought. He hesitated. He said, 'Die Rechnung…' and actually rubbed his finger and thumb together like the comedian they'd seen in the night-club in the summer.

'How much?' said Nicholson bluntly. 'Wieviel?'

The doctor inclined his head self-effacingly. 'For me ... it is egal.' He darted a look at them. 'Siebzig Mark?' When Nicholson whistled he went on, 'Here is privat, eh? Not too much...' He switched to German to complete the suggestion.

Nicholson said, 'Fünfzig?'

The doctor shrugged. 'Also, the sisters make a small note for the pflegekosten. Not so much.'

Nicholson grunted. Pickup nudged him inquisitively. Nicholson muttered, 'Pay up and no questions asked – if he's saying what I think he's saying.'

In the office the young nun wrote out a careful bill for RM 9.75. Watery eyes brightening, the doctor settled for an English five-pound note that Linné had left them. Nicholson, counting the remaining Reichsmarks in his wallet asked how a taxi might be obtained. The nun looked doubtful. The doctor said something to her and she smiled, a delighted smile that broke her shiny round face into many creases. The doctor applied himself to putting it into English. Pickup knew somehow that he was going to offer to take them himself, and felt heartened and excited; suddenly things seemed to be going right again–

'If you will wait ten or fifteen minuten, eh?'

Of course, of course. Professional again now the money was stowed away, he waved aside their thanks and creaked off along the passage. Pickup's optimism was replaced, or at any rate joined, by a return of nervous impatience. The dull acceptance of the accident and its aftermath evaporated. He was fidgeting to be off. Supposing they had just missed a train because the doctor still had something to do in his potty little hospital–

Nick was dressed in his own things except for a terrible shirt they'd found for him, striped with a great big floppy collar. His jacket was stained with blood but it had dried brown and didn't show so much now. They insisted on his sitting in a wheel chair to be pushed along to the hall, and wrapped a blanket round him until at last there was the sound of the doctor's car, and a little toot from his horn, in the courtyard outside. They got Nick into the back seat. It was a saloon, Pickup couldn't see what make. He sat next to Nick and in access of affection and sympathy put an arm awkwardly round his shoulders as if to steady him on the journey. He said, trying to be light-hearted about it, 'At least we've got a good excuse now for not getting back to Cambridge on time.'

'What is that?' said the doctor. He drove for the most part in silence but seemed to be impelled, every minute or two, to prepare and launch some remark which started out confidently only to peter out into vague noises and sawings of one hand. 'Your mister Chamberlain ... here in München...'

'Oh yes,' said Pickup politely. But whatever the doctor had wanted to say was beyond his confidence in himself as a linguist. On the Dachauerstrasse again they passed two marching troupes carrying embroidered standards, one headed by drummers. The doctor said, 'Today, much ... er...' and relapsed into silence.

He was threading his way laterally through the northern parts of the city. They crossed the canal and then the Isar. Nicholson was peering through the windscreen. He tried to direct the doctor who nodded his head vigorously to indicate he knew the way. Then Nicholson was saying, 'Stop, stop,' and they were pulling up in a quiet, dank street. Pickup shared the doctor's puzzlement: only a high wall, not the entrance to any house, much less the vons and zus. But Nicholson was pushing himself out of the car – of course! It was the side door by the summer house. Would it be open though? He saw Nicholson stealthily try it and heard the creak of the hinges and saw against the dank of the wall a crack of paler sky. 'We're in luck,' Nicholson whispered.

The doctor had got out of the car to help with Nick. It looked as if he expected to come in with them. Pickup took Nick's arm. Nicholson held out his hand and declared thanks. The doctor hesitated for a moment, then said, 'Ach, so,' and evidently washing his hands of the matter, folded himself back into his car. As it began to move more away Pickup felt Nick sag against him and heard Nicholson's whispered, 'Watch out.'

Somehow they got him into the summer house. 'Nick. Nick, what is it?' said Pickup.

'He's gone again,' said Nicholson. 'He'll be all right in a minute.'

In the gloom they stumbled against the junk that was stored there. The archery target fell over with a thud. Pickup felt Nick's weight dragging him down but managed to free a hand and flick his cigarette lighter on for a moment. In its gleam Nicholson found the old hammock seat and lugged it clear. They lowered Nick on to it. He said quite clearly, 'Where is this?' but when they said, 'Are you all right now?' there was no reply.

'He's not unconscious or anything, actually,' said Nicholson.

'He's shivering,' said Pickup.

'He'll be O.K. soon,' said Nicholson again. He got to his feet. 'See if you can find something to put over him.'

'Where are you going?'

'To try and get help.'

'Who? – not Jill?'

'Helmuth if I can find him.'

'*Helmuth?* – but we promised not to involve him in our job No link between his part and ours. That was the plan.'

'Things,' said Nicholson, 'have rather departed from the plan.'

Pickup was left alone, but for Nick, in the deepening gloom.

# CHAPTER 9

'As soon as Ian comes back,' Pickup whispered for about the fifteenth time – but when *would* he be back? It seemed hours already. The summer house was cold and clammy and smelled of mould. He'd propped Nick up on some old cushions and covered him with a piece of dusty carpet he'd found. Sometimes the huddled figure mumbled to itself, at other times spoke in that conversational, ordinary way. What had happened to that little bottle of brandy he'd had in his pocket? He'd had it still on the bus, he was sure. Pickup felt a wave of hatred and resentment, that he should have got them all in this mess, and afterwards was ashamed of it. His anxiety was now a dull, dragging one, like when someone was ill, with – on top of the old fears – a curious, irrational unease at lurking in the dark on the vons and zus' property. He glanced nervously at an upstairs light in the house, just visible through the trees and the cracked cobwebby glass of the pavilion. He was cold. His mouth was dry and sore. He tried to wriggle more deeply into the tweedness of his jacket and when that failed resumed a stealthy pacing of the floor. Five – no, ten more times to and fro – and he'd hear a car outside the wall, the peppy note of Helmuth's little B.M.W., the door softly opening and closing, friendly, chaffing voices–

*What was that?* Something in the garden... Pickup shrank into the darkest corner. An apparition, pale, ghostly, rustling. He realised who it was fractionally before she spoke.

'Nick, where are you?'

He said, 'In here, Jill.'

'Where's Nick?'

Nick answered.

'Oh Nick, darling.' She was down by his side in the gloom, careless of her dress. Then, as her eyes adjusted and she saw the bandages, *'Nick!* What have you done?'

Nick said, 'Nothing much.' His voice was croaky, though.

Pickup said, 'The doctor said it wouldn't show too badly, his hair would grow over it.'

'God, does it hurt?' And without waiting for an answer, 'What's it all about, what have you been up to? Was this your idea, Michael?'

'No,' he started to protest, but she'd just noticed Nick's bandaged hand and was exclaiming afresh at that.

Nick said, 'Leave it.'

She took the other hand, stroking it, warming it.

Pickup said, 'How did you know?'

'Ian phoned the house.'

'He was supposed to be–'

'Couldn't find him so he tried me in the end. It was all right, said he was from the consulate or something. They didn't notice anything. I told him some places he might get hold of Helmuth and nipped out.' She sat back on her heels. Bracelets tinkled on her arms. Pickup smelled her perfume. She said, 'What's going to happen?'

'We need Helmuth to get us to the station.'

'There isn't a train until the sleeper.'

'A train anywhere, as long as it gets us out.'

She bent close to Nick again. 'But will Nick be able to? Nick, will you?' And when he didn't answer at once, *'Nickie'*

'Yes': far away.

'What is it?'

'I'm all right.'

'Does it hurt?'

'A bit.'

She looked at Pickup. Even in the dark he could tell it was an accusing look. 'How can he travel? He ought to be in bed.'

'We have to go. Didn't Ian explain?'

'No.' But she didn't seem to want to find out now. She said, 'He's cold.'

'Could you pinch a rug or something from the house?'

'I'll see.' She straightened up effortlessly. Now you could see she was wearing a dinner dress, with some sort of stiff silky thing draped round her shoulders. Nick was mumbling something. 'What is it, Nickie? A drink? I'll find one for you, I promise.' She said to Pickup, 'Don't go away,' and slipped into the garden again and vanished like a white moth.

She was back sooner than Pickup had dared hope. She put a cushion behind Nick's head and tucked a blanket round him.

'Drink,' said Nick.

'I could only find Kummel.'

'Doesn't matter.' There was the sound of the stopper coming out, and then Nick sighing in extravagant satisfaction.

'Perhaps Michael would like some.'

'No, it's all right.' Beer is what he would have liked, or whisky and soda. He saw it glowing in his father's bulbous tumbler, the little bubbles rising in strings to the surface. Sometimes at Christmas or on his first night back from anywhere he would be given one, too. His parents! He was swamped with sudden remorse, God, how his mother would WORRY if she knew ... supposing they never saw him again. His eyes smarted again.

At last there was the noise of a motor, then the garden door being cautiously opened. Pickup said, 'Here they are.'

Helmuth said, 'Ah, Nick, how are you? We must bite on the bullet.' He sounded unperturbed. He switched on an electric torch and lifted the edge of the head bandage and said, 'Oh yes, quite a little cut.' Nick grunted but did not open his visible eye.

'What's up. Helmuth? Will you tell me if nobody else will?'

'I don't know that I may—'

'Do you think I don't have a pretty good idea? Something to do with your precious Klaus and that camp?'

No one replied.

'I might have known it. You stupid bloody fools.'

Helmuth said equably, 'The main thing is to get the fellows away before too much is found out. And you, my dear – should you not be thinking of your dinner engagement?'

'Blow my dinner engagement!'

'If you are missing they will become curious in the house. Also, Kurt's parents will be very sad if anyone should spoil their table plan on what is such a proud evening for them.' The irony was gentle.

'And blow Kurt's parents.' But she looked distractedly towards the house. She turned to them again. 'Are you sure the sleeper won't do? Then at least he'd be comfortable.'

Nicholson said, 'It's cutting it fine.'

Pickup blurted out what had occurred to him earlier and been suppressed again. 'The roll-call in the morning is not until six, is it? Even if they found anyone missing straight-away, by the time they'd put two and two together about the generator and got on to BHL and found out about us and got a message to the frontiers, surely it would be eight o'clock anyway ... I mean, the sleeper ought to be all right–' though even as he said it, he felt the dread of more hours of waiting.

'I thought you were the one who was so

anxious to get back, Mickup.'

'I am, but...'

Helmuth said, 'I think it would be not so dangerous.' Even for Helmuth he sounded astonishingly casual.

Jill said, 'It would make all the difference, Ian.'

Nicholson replied after perhaps two full seconds. 'If that's what you all feel, then of course.'

'I'll get back before then, plead a headache if necessary. Look after him, won't you?'

'I say!'

'Yes.'

'We could do with a little more money if you could find some.'

'I'll try.' She was gone.

Nicholson said, 'I wish that when we'd decided something you wouldn't want to alter it every time. Just because a girl you've got a crush on rolls her eyes at you.'

'It wasn't that—'

'Furthermore, did you have to spill all that stuff about roll-calls and generators and what-have-you in front of the same girl just when she's about to dine at the Four Seasons Hotel with her Nazi friends?'

Pickup was silent. 'Nicholson was so un-fair—'

Helmuth said, 'Actually I must tell you that it is possible you will have nothing to fear on your journey, you may sleep the whole way.'

'What do you mean?'

'If there is no escape from Dachau then they will be looking for no one.'

Nicholson said harshly, 'I don't see.'

'Today there were a number of releases from the camp; others were transported in a body to another place, we think maybe Buchenwald – you have told me you saw them yourselves. A student at the university who boarded the train at Allach also saw them and thinks that he perhaps recognised Klaus. He could not be sure, he was not among his class.'

Nicholson said, 'I'm sorry, Helmuth.'

'Me too,' said Pickup, his mind racing to consider the possibilities.

'It is I that should be saying he is sorry. All the dangers you have faced – poor Nick's torn head – if it should all be for nothing.' He studied the luminous dial of the big pilot's chronometer on his wrist. 'Naturally I must keep my rendezvous, whether the other may keep it or no.' He paused. 'I don't suppose either of you would wish to come with me. It would not be so lonely.'

Pickup said, 'I'll come if you like.' He heard his voice, flat and matter-of-fact, as if coming from a loudspeaker in his head. The words were familiar, as if he'd already uttered them. 'That is, if Ian doesn't mind.'

'Whatever next, Mickup?' The note of surprise was laid on thickly. 'No, of course, I don't mind. As long as you're back in time.'

'We shall be back immediately,' said Helmuth. 'Good! Then it is settled. Thank you, Michael.'

Why, why had he done it? As he squirmed into the little B.M.W. alongside Helmuth Pickup tried to convince himself: because of bloody Nicholson and his sneering ways: because anything was better than that waiting: because it was flattering to be taken along by Helmuth; because he'd never ridden in the B.M.W; because he alone had not yet come face to face with das Reich, as Nick and Phil and even Nicholson, before the Feldherrnhalle, had come face to face with it; because, deep down, he'd somehow known all along that the stunt had begun and ended that morning, nothing else would happen, there wouldn't be an escape.

In London Rolf Ehrlich was writing a letter.

He wore his long overcoat for the gas fire in his room was not lit. By his side was a flagon of Australian burgundy and a cheap glass. He had written so far.

For me to thank you for your many kindnesses may strike you as illogical. It is not. I am truly appreciative of all that you and other of your countrymen have done for a stranger in their midst. If I have neglected offers both of friendship and employment it is because of the duty I have felt to complete that poor manuscript now in your possession which you have generously agreed to bring to the notice of a publisher. I leave to you, or to him, the form in which it shall appear. I am concerned only that it *should* appear, that the world may learn something of what, under Hitler, German can do to German. Should any profit be made, let it benefit that cause of yours which has helped me and many fellow victims.

He drained his glass and refilled it, and for the moment did not resume his task.

Helmuth switched off the ignition; there was only the sound of the springs creaking and the whirr of the tyres as the little car continued to coast. He'd already turned out the lights and he had to hold his door half open and peer into the dark to keep to the edge of the road. Pickup thought they were going to roll on for ever but at last Helmuth steered on to the verge and with a bump, another, and a faint swishing of the petrol in the tank they came to a halt. Helmuth whispered to him and started to get out. Pickup followed suit on his side. There was a thud as the door closed and he felt rather than heard Helmuth's reproving hiss. Together they pushed the two-seater clear of the road. Two hundred, perhaps two hundred and fifty, yards ahead, bathed in the rays of the searchlights, was the bleak grey wall of KZ Dachau.

Helmuth had driven straight through the town, crossed the river and made a detour round the northern perimeter of the district before recrossing the Amper to approach the camp from Prittlbach. It was a dark night though not as inky black as they'd all hoped. The rain had stopped and a cold breeze blew in their faces. Helmuth sniffed it and murmured, 'Winter is on her way. Not too long before we ski again, eh?' Somewhere, it could have been in the camp or the barracks beyond, a dog was howling.

They got back into the car. Pickup could hear the ticking of the dashboard clock. They watched the ragged spread of light from a searchlight slowly moved along the wall. It came from a tower in the middle of the wall over to their right, hidden by trees. The next nearest tower was along the side wall – by which the road ran – but a good quarter of a mile away. Pickup saw vividly in his mind's eye the model he and Stanley had so laboriously built and that corner of the balsa wall over which Philipp Linné had so carelessly jumped his fingers as he remarked that this was the least well covered ... all being well he was safely in Switzerland now while Pickup was parked a thirty-seconds' dash from that very corner–

He heard Helmuth swear softly. On them before they'd heard or seen anything a cyclist creaked past, glancing curiously at the white car reflected in the dim radiance of his acetylene lamp.

Helmuth said, 'If you were a young lady it would look more natural, you know ... *Moment!*' He unknotted the silk square he wore round his neck and gave it to Pickup. 'Round the head, like a girl, eh?'

'What?' He didn't see–

'Like so.' Helmuth demonstrated.

'Do I have to?'

'*Please.* It is not for a joke.'

The square was smooth and heavy and smelled of cologne. He tied it under his chin.

'Very nice.'

Helmuth shifted his position and he felt an arm round his shoulders, drawing him close. By God, suppose Helmuth was a homo or something and thought he was one, too! He resisted,

'Michael, do as I ask.'

He let himself relax against the collar of Helmuth's leather coat. He could smell its school-satchel smell mixed with the perfume of the cologne.

'So,' said Helmuth. 'No German would disturb two lovers, Now we may even have a cigarette.'

Pickup found his cigarettes and they lit up carefully, smoking them in cupped hands. Helmuth looked for the hundredth time at the ghostly green hands of his watch and leaning forward fiddled under the dashboard. There was a snatch of music, very faint, a distorted squeaking sound, then a voice in German. Helmuth listened for a minute before switching off again. He said, 'Tonight there is only one news.'

'What's that?'

'In Paris Third Secretary vom Rath has died.'

'The one who was shot?'

'Yes. He was only a young fellow, you know. It will be hard for his parents.'

'I'm sorry.'

'But that is not all. He was killed by a Jew. I do not like it.'

'What can happen?'

Helmuth squeezed Pickup's shoulders and sighed. 'I do not know. But I am a München-er. We are more – more temperamental than other Germans. We learn to have antennae, eh? We can feel what is in the air, and driving through the city tonight I felt a *hochspannung*. You know what *hochspannung* means? It is high force in electricity'– he pointed with the butt of his concealed cigarette – 'as in the wire fence before us.'

'High tension,' said Pickup.

'That is correct: high tension. Well, so is the atmosphere in Munich tonight. Of course we have all the big boys in town. The Fuhrer himself dines at the old Council House – have you ever seen our Hitler, Michael?'

'No.'

'I have seen him twice. His eyes are very

strange. They seem to burn, you know.' He pondered. 'Let us say that is fortunate your friend Philipp is already gone.'

'What do you mean?'

'He is Jew, is he not?'

'I've never heard such a thing.'

Helmuth's glowing cigarette described a dismissive arc. 'For me it is equal. But here one always hears that the family is some way Jewish. The father was a big supporter of Hitler at one time, you know. He called himself von Linné then.'

'Well I think it's a lot of silly nonsense.' But he remembered nudges and veiled allusions of Nicholson's and even Nick's, and Linné rubbing his wrist in the hotel room after the Feldherrnhalle business, and a million miles away, a million years before, Paddy Hutton going on about them – he said, 'He hasn't got a hooked nose.'

Helmuth laughed. 'You should not believe our nice cartoons. But ... well, he is the one of you who is safely home, eh?'

'It wasn't his idea.'

'No?'

'And anyway, who went right into the camp and fixed the thing and–'

'Nicholas also. But I agree, it was not the deed of a coward. Nor are you a coward,

Michael, to keep this appointment with me.'

He fell silent. Pickup had a sudden desire to be rid of his cigarette. In the darkness he couldn't see an ashtray. There was a flap in the side-screen. He pushed the cigarette out, wincing as his clumsiness made a little shower of sparks. If Helmuth noticed he said nothing. Pickup said, 'How much longer now?' He heard Helmuth start to say, 'only two min–'

Without warning, without a flicker, the lights went out. In their abrupt extinction all was inky black. Pickup shut his eyes to try and clear them of green patterns branded on the retina. He found himself saying, 'It must have been fast.'

'But there was no roar.'

'What roar?'

'Of the bomb.'

Pickup couldn't believe what he heard. Was his leg being pulled, at a time like this! 'You don't mean – you didn't really think – they didn't explain?'

'I don't know what you mean.'

'It wasn't a bomb, ever! It's an automatic time switch that Phil and Nick wired into the circuit. You know, they're used in factories and places to turning the heating off and on...'

'I did not know, I did not know. Truly I did not. The Infernal Machine–'

'That was only joke name. Well, I suppose it was a sort of code name as well.'

'Of course, of course. It is much better, it is altogether much better. I see that now. I am simple!' He laughed with the relief of it.

'The beauty of it is that we've set it to go on again after twenty minutes, so with luck they won't bother trying to find out what went wrong until the morning. You know, by the time they get anyone along there–'

'*Moment!*' Helmuth freed his arm and gently opening his door, listened.

Pickup heard the dog again and – was that a shout? He became aware of an halation in the distance, a growing blur of light which at that instant hardened and became specific and drew nearer. The rays made patterns on the windscreen of the B.M.W., shone fitfully inside – from the corner of his eye he could see Helmuth's profile, quenched of colour. Even as he cringed down in his seat, clawing off the silk square, he thought, It's only headlights and next minute the lorry was rumbling past.

In the restored darkness he whispered, 'Can we go?'

'*Psst.*'

He was suddenly, overwhelmingly frightened. *'Please.'*

Helmuth stared into the dark. He reached
for his torch, switched it on, pointing low,
half-masked by his hand. *Out there something
was approaching, gasping, grunting.* Helmuth
had his door wide open – someone arrived!
Went crashing, honking, thrust by Helmuth
into the space behind the seats. The starter
whirred, the engine was suddenly deafen-
ing, then he was flung against Helmuth as
Helmuth hauled the little car round in a U-
turn to accelerate away after the retreating
lorry, the way they'd come.

Ehrlich had completed his letter. He folded
it into an envelope and propped it on the
mantelpiece alongside a small pile of
shillings. He crossed to the wash-basin. It
contained old newspapers which had been
soaking in water. He squeezed out one of
the sodden messes and began to seal the
cracks around his window. When that was
done he turned to the door. For the large
gap beneath the door he rolled up the little
square of carpet. He poured another glass of
wine before fetching blankets and the pillow
from his bed and arranging them before the
fireplace. He placed the burgundy within

reach, and a bowl in case he should feel sick. Still in his overcoat he crouched down and began to insert the shillings in the meter.

'Did anyone see him or shout or run after him, anything like that?'

Helmuth translated Nicholson's question and returned the answer. 'He believes not.'

'Shine the torch a second.'

Helmuth kept his hand over the lens so that only a little light escaped into the summer house. It was just enough for Pickup to make out an animal face blinking and shuddering: shaven, thick-lipped, snouty, somehow familiar. He also saw striped baggy clothing torn in two places, a blood-stained rag round one hand, great boots.

'He's only a kid,' said Nicholson.

'He says he worked by Klaus. They were going to come together until Klaus was moved – only today! It is terrible to have missed him so shortly.'

'What was he in for?'

'He is Bible student. They are a kind of religious believer, you know.'

'I suppose that's better than a Jew or a bum-boy. What's the matter with him?'

'I do not understand.'

'Shaking like that.'

'For heaven's sake,' said Pickup. 'He's been through it.'

'What shall we do with him?' said Helmuth. In the leaking torchlight the sculpted profile had become gaunt and hollow. The sweptback hair was disarranged and Pickup fancied he could see a thinning spot on top. Nicholson was rattled out of his soldierly calm, too. He jingled some loose change in his pocket and his voice had an even jaggeder edge.

He said, 'Didn't you have anything worked out?'

'For Klaus there were plans, naturally. But for this boy...'

'There's nothing *we* can do. The moment Jill is back we're off – or before that, if she's much longer.'

Pickup said, 'We can't just abandon him.'

'You do not understand, Michael,' said Helmuth. 'When they discover about him, which will be' – he looked at his watch – 'in six or seven hours at the most, they will hunt him with dogs, turn out troops, barricade roads, close frontiers, occupy rail stations. They will be *mad* for him.'

'But having let so many go yesterday, and transferred others – isn't there a chance they might not notice?'

Helmuth shook his head impatiently. 'You do not know we Germans.'

'It seems such – such a waste of the whole stunt.'

'Stunt? – what is that?'

'You were a stunt flyer, weren't you?'

Helmuth switched off the torch. 'Oh yes, but that was children's play beside this kind of stunt.'

Pickup shivered. There was silence until it was broken by Nick, who mumbled something thickly and then, more loudly, 'Who's that? Who've you got there?'

'Did you give him that bottle?' said Nicholson irritably.

'No, Jill did.'

'He's half drunk already.'

Pickup said, 'Perhaps we could give him some clothes at least.'

'Who?'

The ... boy there.'

'Our luggage is all at the station.'

'How are we supposed to be getting to the station?'

Helmuth said, 'You know my car is only a little sport one–'

Nicholson said. 'If that girl gets back she said something about sneaking the vons and zus' old crate. She knows where the keys are kept.'

'Ian?'

'Yep?'

'That sleeper isn't going to get us out early enough, is it?'

'You might have thought of that earlier, instead of letting yourself be talked round by that flibbertigibbet.'

'What I'm getting at is that if we're going to sneak the car at all we might as well sneak it properly. What's to stop us driving now for the nearest frontier?'

Nicholson thought it over. He said, 'We couldn't very well leave her to face the music. She'd have to come too.'

'I agree.'

'Would she, though?'

'If she thought Nicholas needed her,' said Helmuth.

'Then Nicholas is bloody well going to need her.'

# CHAPTER 10

The red glow was getting nearer. Pickup judged it might come from somewhere in the posh Residenz quarter. He glanced sideways at Nicholson but Nicholson was concentrating on mastering the Horch and following the white sports car ahead. Helmuth had insisted on piloting them through the city and it was rather a good idea, because he could also act as a last long-stop and telephone Linné or the Consul or both if anything happened. Furthermore, in the narrow space behind the seats of the B.M.W., beneath an old tarpaulin, cowered the fugitive, thus freeing them for the moment of his damning presence.

On their way at last! Pickup had felt the thrill of relief, of security even, he'd used to feel as a boy when his mother had settled herself in the front of the Wolseley Hornet with rug and Thermos and paper handkerchiefs and Vapex and his father had made sure all the windows and doors of the house were shut and they were finally, actually, on

their way to the Lakes or to his grand-
parents for Christmas, isolated in their own
little moving world. At the same time a
horrid dragging sort of tightness was still
there inside him. The red glow in the sky
was both exciting and disquieting. With its
maroon coachwork and little crests on the
doors the old Horch was pretty conspic-
uous. If anyone had seen it go ... and there
was still the luggage to collect.

One thing they needn't have worried
about: Jill. She'd rustled back curiously subdued, asking Helmuth what was going on in
the town, shaking her head at his protective
reassurances though without saying anything
more. She'd listened to their whispered
proposals without comment and looked at
the gibbering fugitive as if hardly noticing
him. Kneeling down by Nick in his vague
drunken pain she'd said, 'You've been going
it, haven't you?' and then in a louder voice,
to no one in particular, 'All right. I'll shove
some things together.' She'd returned later
in her fur coat, holding one small case still
uncommunicative as they pushed the Horch
out of the coach-house and round to the
garden door.

They were leaving the quieter streets by
the English Garden. Late trams clanged

along the Prinzregentenstrasse. A Mercedes limousine, pennant fluttering, bore some Nazi big-wig to the Führerhaus or the Feldherrnhalle – it must have been nearly midnight; the S.S. recruits were about to be sworn in. At midnight! That was a melodramatic touch for you. He turned to look at Jill but she sat expressionless. He turned back. You could see the flames from the fire now, beyond them the dark bulk of the cathedral just discernible against the sky. At last the broad expanse of the Bahnhofsplatz lay before them. Pickup tensed himself as Helmuth led the way round to the lighted, flag-hung façade of the station. He pounded up the steps with the receipts ready in his hand, jiffled impatiently while the left-luggage man peered at them as if he'd never seen such items before, struggled back with a case in each hand, another under his arm, Nick's umbrella – who else would have brought an umbrella! – hooked precariously over a wrist.

Nicholson, who could have helped him, you'd have thought, was standing in the open for anyone to see, staring across the square at the burning building. Flames were shooting from the roof now and – at this instant – a fountain of sparks that slowed and swirled and hung in the smoky air. Pickup yelled at him and started to throw the stuff any old how into the car. People were coming away from the fire, passing by with strange blank expressions. He briefly registered fire-engines, the green uniforms of police. Helmuth, who'd parked sixty or seventy yards ahead of them, was crawling forward again. He shouted again as Nicholson strolled back with an infuriating, 'All right, Mickup, don't panic.'

As they turned into the Bayerstrasse he said, 'What was it, then?'

'Synagogue,' said Nicholson,

Nick came to life. 'What about it, what about a synagogue?'

'It's burning.'

'That's all right then.' His breath filled the car with the stink of alcohol and caraway.

Jill said, 'It had just started when I left the Viejahreszeiten.'

Pickup glanced back at her. There was a strain, a breaking quality to that clipped voice he hadn't heard before.

Nicholson said, 'And it looks as if it's not the only one.' Another fire flickered on the skyline to the south. They passed a column of stormtroopers marching behind a stand-ard bearer. They saw a shattered shop-window, it could only have been moments earlier for lights were springing on in upper windows above and there was a glimpse of figures clattering down a side-street, a bobbing torch and as the scene was left behind the explosion and cascading tinkle of another one. Wedged amid the luggage Pickup felt a secret shameful elation. These were other people in other trouble: people who didn't concern them in their enclosed, fleeing world; trouble, he knew instinctively, that might distract attention from their trouble–

Nicholson was slowing down. Though there was little traffic in the street a tram in front of them was only inching forward and the space on its inside was blocked by a parked lorry. They would be two or three miles west of the station, somewhere round Pasing from what Pickup remembered of the map. Helmuth wasn't in sight. He must have slipped past while it was still possible. The tram stopped altogether. Nicholson pulled out to try and get through in the centre of the street but it was thronged with booted, brown-shirted stormtroopers. Others were spilling from a lorry which had drawn up to add to the congestion. Two men were hammering on the front door of a tall thin block, stepping back to shout hoarsely, then hammering again.

He heard Jill catch her breath. From another doorway, a woman, another, two children, a man were thrust into the glare of headlights and torches. Against the brown uniforms and everyday drab of the lorries their night-clothes made them look like exotic hunted birds. The first woman was just a girl and, Pickup saw with a pang, a pretty one: long dark hair, white face, huge frightened eyes. He could see her blue pyjamas and fluffy slippers below her outdoor coat. A thug in brown shoved her towards the lorry. The smaller child's face was screwed up in tears. The bigger one, a boy, held her hand and tried to calm her. The second woman, who was big and fat with a nightdress billowing under her coat, started towards them, then turned as another man came stumbling out into the glare. He was old and tripped and went sprawling.

Everything happened very quickly after that. The first man ran forward and one of the stormtroopers hit him and he went down. The woman was screaming. Pickup saw someone lash out at her, too; she warded off the blow with an arm and then another stormtrooper had grabbed at her and wrenched her coat half off and ripped her nightdress down and a great white breast was sagging out, but she didn't care and just struggled to get to the man who was trying to get up from the pavement with blood on his face–

Above the din of screaming and jeering he heard Jill. 'Christ. we've got to do something.'

'Stay where you are,' snapped Nicholson.

'Let me out.' She struggled with the door.

'Shut up!'

'The bastards,' said Nick loudly, 'the bastards, we'll show 'em.'

'For God's sake stop him, Mickup.'

Pickup grabbed at his door lock. Nicholson was snatching at the gears of the Horch. As Pickup twisted round again he raced the engine, blared the horn and nosed forward. Pickup saw a raised hand, heard hoarse voices, saw brown shorts, peaked oblong caps and a scowling pink face thrust low to stare at him through the side window. Then suddenly they were moving faster, with only a parting thump from a fist on the body-work they were clear–

Nicholson breathed out noisily. In the distance were Helmuth's waiting rear-lights.

They pulled off the road a few miles outside the city. In their headlights Helmuth looked more drawn than ever. No one spoke at first. Helmuth had the kid with him, shivering in Nicholson's trench coat. Underneath it he was naked except for his boots. They'd made him strip off the incriminating Dachau garb while they were waiting for Jill. It was buried now under the floor of the summer house. Pickup rummaged in his case for a shirt and pants, both used. Nicholson, who was of the nearest build, donated a pair of worsted trousers. They raided Nick's stuff for a pullover. Pickup hesitated for a moment, then emptied the pockets of his sports coat and slipped on the black jacket instead.

The kid eyed the clothes and shook his head and said something to Helmuth.

'What's the matter now?' asked Nicholson.

'Oh, he is a little worried. It is nothing.' For the first time Pickup had ever noticed he pronounced a 'w' like a 'v'.

'Well, tell him to get the clothes on, and hurry. I'd like my macintosh back.'

Pickup wondered if he was shy in front of Jill but Jill had sat down on the running board of the Horch and was smoking a cigarette and staring at the ground.

'Come on.' He tugged at the coat.

The kid undid the buttons and ducked down behind the shelter of the car to slip it off. Pickup saw a stocky but what seemed, in the dim illumination of the side-lights, an almost femininely smooth white body – except for shadowy marks on the bottom. Pickup looked away, forced himself to look again. As the kid moved Pickup glimpsed an awful discolouration, raised weals. He swung round in dismay towards the others but they were engrossed in whispered consultation. Helmuth was opening a map on the Horch's bonnet, Nicholson was counting up what Pickup recognised as petrol coupons.

He said, 'There's the money, too. What's it cost again?'

'We worked out it was about three and six a gallon,' said Pickup.

Nicholson whistled. Helmuth pinned the map down with his torch and peered into the car to consult the gauge. He said, 'I think you will perhaps be all right with the spare can. There are not so many pumps open at night. Also, it is good the less you are noticed...'

The kid had got Nicholson's trousers on

now. Jill was still sitting on the running board, head down, the cigarette burning in her hand.

Pickup said, 'Maybe we could make Nick more comfy.'

She looked up. There were tears on her face. 'I'm sorry, I didn't mean to—'

'It's all right. If we could make a sort of bed on the back seat...'

When they looked inside he'd been sick. Pickup felt his stomach turn. Jill mopped it up and said, 'You were going it, weren't you?'

'I'm sorry.' It was only a whisper. He didn't sound drunk any longer.

'Never mind. Are the stitches hurting?'

'They feel so ... *big.*'

'I found some aspirins.'

He took them greedily. He said, 'I wasn't dreaming, was I? Those people in the street...!'

'No. Forget it now. Try and sleep.'

The seat wasn't wide enough for a bed but they slewed him round so he could be half reclining with his head and shoulders on the faded velvet cushions the Freiin kept in the car, and his legs diagonally across the well. His breath was awful.

The kid was fully dressed now, and much

more like a human being except for his shaven head. There wasn't much you could do about that unless – Pickup remembered a beret he had stuffed in the pocket of his mac, and gave him that. The kid pulled it on awkwardly. Who was it he reminded him of? Of course: Stanley was older and blotchier but had that same snouty look. He was religious, too.

O Lord, was it a sign? And if so, of what? He busied himself heaving the cases on the luggage rack at the back of the Horch. It would give them more room inside. The strap was enormously thick and stiff and dirty and he had to put his foot against the buckle and pull with all his weight to engage the prong.

'What are you doing?' called Nicholson.

'Putting the luggage on the rack.'

He heard Jill talking to the kid, and his halting replies.

'Hurry up.' It was Nicholson's voice again. 'It's time we were off.'

'Coming.'

Helmuth was folding up his map. Nicholson was stowing his trench-coat somewhere by the driving seat. Pickup nerved himself, He said, 'What about the kid?'

'That's up to him. Give him ten marks if

you like.'

'I think we should take him.'

'What on earth for?'

'The farther he can get from the camp the better, obviously.'

'He comes from near Stuttgart, his name's Emil, he worked for an architect,' said Jill in her flat voice, 'And he wants to go back to Dachau.'

'*What?*'

'He's in a hell of a state, poor kid. Says he should never have escaped. It was God's will that he was sent there–'

Helmuth said, 'He has already told me the same. I did not tell you because...' He shrugged.

Nicholson said, 'And of all the poor sods in there we had to pluck him!'

Pickup said, 'We can't let him go back. We can't I – I saw what they've done to him already.'

'You heard what he said.'

'He doesn't know what he's saying,' said Jill.

'Anyway, there isn't room for him.'

'We'll make room.'

Nicholson was silent, There were two little seats that hinged down from the division.

Pickup proposed that he and the kid

should take them while Jill went in the front. She shook her head and said she needed to be with Nick. Pickup said, 'I'll keep you company.' They bundled the kid into the front. They shook hands with Helmuth and Jill embraced him. No one spoke much, but Helmuth tapped on the window as Nicholson started the engine and when Pickup wound it down, stuck his head in. There'd been something else he meant to say.

'About what we passed on Bodenseestrasse ... the S.A., you know, are the old party fighters from when there was much fighting to be done. We do not see so much of them now. This is their great night of the year.' He blinked. 'You must only remember that not all Germans will be proud of them in the next days.'

Nicholson said, 'Don't worry. They can burn down what they like, beat up who they like, and smash every window in the Reich as long as it keeps 'em too busy to notice us. I'll be happy to hear tinkling glass all night.' He eased the Horch on to the road,

Looking back at Helmuth as he was lost in the darkness Pickup knew, and felt, and could hardly bear, his loneliness.

# CHAPTER 11

Jill's hand in his was soft and responsive, answering pressure for gentle pressure, stroke for stroke of finger even when she slept, as if it had a life – and love – of its own. At other times he would relax his hand and hers would lie cool and dormant on his palm. His arm was round her and she rested her head against his shoulder but it was the communion of the hands that made up for the numbness in his bottom from the hard little tip-up seat and the pins and needles in the leg he had jammed awkwardly under the rear seat. The fragrance of her hair was lost in the smell of hot oil and leather and sourness and stuffiness which filled the car. Through the rear screen the vague shapes of trees and clouds whirled away, occasionally the flash and dwindling red tail-lamps of another vehicle. For a while the road bordered a lake. Nick slept. If he turned his head as much as he could without disturbing Jill he could see the kid Emil's head lolling in sleep, too, and from the corner of his eye the lighted dials of the dashboard and Nicholson's hand on the wheel and the blurred beginnings of Nicholson's profile.

Already the speeding, private world had worked its spell. Nothing outside the misted windows could touch them. The events of the day had frozen into glossy pictures like the photographs outside a cinema. Even the Jewish family, the wide-eyed girl, the woman whose great white breast hung out – for the moment he was numbed. He was mostly conscious of an indefined sorrow for everyone, and a sharper one for the girl who leaned against him. For all her flippancy she was the one who'd – who'd *cared* more about this country and now she must be feeling absolutely beaten.

When she was awake once, or might have been awake, he said: 'You know, there are people who simply wouldn't believe you if you tried to tell what you'd seen. I've a friend called Paddy Hutton who's at sea and wouldn't believe a word of it. He's got an aunty here–' he said it *anty* in his joke northern accent– 'and he thinks it's marvellous. And the funny thing is that though he left school after school cert. and doesn't read much or anything, when he talked about it he made it sound the most exciting

273

place in the world. He had this swastika pennant on his bike and someone wanted to beat him up for it once, I think it must have been a Red.'

In a town something was burning and there were plate glass windows shattered in the square.

'They're bullies, aren't they? Bucks we used to call them at home, I don't know why. If you wore a prep school blazer they'd chase you across the sandhills. There were miles of sandhills then with cottages and a wood and a big empty house, they're all built over now. I used to be petrified of them until one day they caught me and I saw they were just ordinary kids from the Parade School. Same thing at school: went in fear and trembling of the louts until one day I realised just how ignorant they were. I was still scared but it was – it was better, then.'

The Horch wasn't at all a bad old bus once you'd got used to her, according to Nicholson: four litres, eight cylinders, could tramp along all right. Helmuth had warned him to look out for overheating but so far it had been O.K.

'There was a story that impressed me terrifically when I was about, oh, ten or eleven. About this brother and sister in France during the war. I can't remember why they lived in France but they did, and Daddy was a lieutenant-colonel in the Argyll and Sutherland Highlanders and there was a picture of them watching him leading the regiment past their house and you could see the letters A. and S.H. on his shoulders. The point was this boy was spoilt and sissy and generally a disappointment to everyone, but his little sister was taken very ill and the only thing was to get her to some hospital in England very quickly. So the R.F.C. provided an aeroplane and Michael – that was the hero's name, which of course was very significant to me – had to go along too and look after her. There was a terrific description of the flight through the night, a bit like us driving through the night now, and he did all the right things and it was The Making of Michael, which is what the book was called. I used to imagine I had a kid sister and invent all sorts of dramatic circumstances in which I would look after her.'

In another town more windows gaped. They heard a marching song.

'Friedrichshafen, here we come. At least, that's where Helmuth was suggesting. All I know about Friedrichshafen is that it's the Zeppelin place. I used to dream about airships, thought aeroplanes were very boring and sort of illogical. I was taken to Cardington and saw the R.101 or maybe it was the R.100. Then the Graf Zeppelin flew over us at home once. Another time there was an exhibition in George Henry Lees or Owen Owens or one of the stores in Liverpool with a kind of imitation of the state-rooms with the tables laid for dinner and everything. The cups and saucers were straw-coloured with gold edges and a little blue crest of a Zeppelin.'

'Are we going to catch a Zeppelin home?'

'Why not?'

They were slowing down. He screwed his head round trying to see.

'What's up?' he asked Nicholson.

'Overheated.'

They stretched their legs and stamped their feet while oily fumes drifted from the raised bonnet. The road had been climbing, Nicholson said, which could account for the trouble. There was a feel of mountains and mountain air. A lorry and trailer which they'd passed a few minutes earlier ground by in thunderous low gear. Pickup glimpsed the driver looking out *through* the spokes of the giant steering wheel; on top of his cab glowed an illuminated yellow triangle.

They set off again. The kid had slept through it all on the front passenger seat. With the beret he looked even more like Stanley. Strange that he was not only religious like Stanley but an apprentice architect as well. How soft and opulent Jill's fur coat was...

He heard snuffling, snoring noises and realised he was making them. His mouth felt slack and wet, his head bulged. He forced his eyes open. He must have drifted off ... for how long? The retreating sky seemed lighter and misty. He watched the headlights of a car on the road behind them. Sometimes they'd be lost as it turned or dipped, then there'd be a faint diffusion in the air, growing milkier until suddenly the two bright sources shone straight at you.

Nicholson seemed to be driving faster, The Horch swayed and rattled – perhaps that had woken him. He reached out a hand to steady them. Nicholson whispered, 'Can you see that car behind us?'

'Yes.'

'Is Jill asleep?'

'I think so. What's the matter?'

'It looks as if we're being followed.'

Behind closed lids Emil strove to know what

he should do. Uncertainty weighed on him. He had hardened his heart and stopped his ears and thought only of himself. He had schemed more deviously than the serpent to creep from his bed leaving it humped into the shape of a sleeping man, and to steal in the shadows from barrack to barrack and then worm his way to that far corner. There, the thought of what he had already done had awed him so much that he could only go on, he dared not go back. Yet the sudden darkness that covered the camp. just as the worldly stranger had whispered would happen – could it not be God-sent? Was it a signal to go and bear witness to which he now turned faint heart? The waiting motor-car, these strange foreigners, who had sent them? He prayed for a sign. He knew only that he feared Jehovah, he feared the guards and more than either he feared the brother whom he had learned to call the block-senior.

The road was dropping again now. Pickup could feel the brakes crying as the heavy car went into each bend. He remained oddly indifferent to the pursuing vehicle, if pursuing it were. For the second time it had fallen back out of sight: yet when Nicholson had slowed his pace because the temperature gauge was rising again it too had slowed, making no attempt to overtake. If its headlights were off there was no way of telling how far behind...

Nicholson said, 'She's boiling again. Too much third gear coming down. I'm going to look for a turning off.'

On the outskirts of a village he braked savagely to a halt and fumbled for reverse. Pickup saw a leaning iron gate, a stone pillar topped by a stone animal. There was the crunch of gravel under the tyres.

Pickup said, 'You're on the grass.'

'Can't help that.' But he straightened up and crept forward a yard before switching off motor and lights.

'What is it?' asked Jill.

'Nothing. There was a car that might have been following.'

Nicholson held his finger to his lips. There was silence except for a low singing noise from the radiator. Wisps of steam escaped from the cap. They were backed into the entrance to some little schloss or something, he couldn't see what. The drive curled away and was lost in the darkness.

Nicholson said, 'There was a fork in the road just ahead. I'm going to see which way he goes – if he goes.' Carefully he opened his door and slithered out. Pickup followed him. The park was a few feet above road level. Nicholson parted the leaves of a bush and they could see the fork only fifty yards away. The morning air was raw. The sound of a motor came muffled at first, then plainer.

It was a middle-sized saloon, of what make Pickup could not tell; fawn or grey in colour. It was slowing down and at the fork it came to a stop, the driver obviously uncertain which road to take. Suddenly the interior light was switched on. The back of the car seemed to be heaped with bright-coloured cushions – or were they clothes? Pickup couldn't see much of the driver but the map he'd been consulting caught the light as he let it drop again. The lamp went out. The car moved off, taking the right fork.

They returned to the parked Horch.

'Where's the kid?' Pickup asked Jill.

'He wanted to pee as far as I could tell. So does Nick if you can give me–'

'Which way did he go?'

Without waiting for an answer he tore to the gateway, looked up and down, spun round to look back into the grounds. Nothing moved. He might have known, he might have known ... what was that? He couldn't hear anything, couldn't see, but was certain the kid was very close. He took a step. A shadow broke from the other shadows and clattered away. Pickup ran and hurled himself. He'd been no great shakes as a rugby player but with a clumsy grip round the kid's waist he brought him to a stop.

Panting, he led him back.

Nicholson stood scowling by the car. He said, 'You needn't have bothered.'

'Look, he hasn't even any money. At least we can give him whatever we have left at the end.' He daren't say that he still hoped for some magic deliverance for them all, including – what was his name? Emil.

That same Emil launched into a hurried, mumbled speech.

Jill translated. 'He is very unhappy about leaving the camp. The Brethren are trusted and he has betrayed them. The Brethren will no longer get the most trustworthy jobs in the camp. He wants us to take him back.'

The kid wrenched himself free of Pickup's grasp to appeal directly to Jill.

Nicholson hit him.

The kid lurched sideways and fell on to his knees. He spat out blood and then fumbled in his mouth with a finger.

'You bastard,' said Pickup. 'What did you want to do that for?' He took a pace towards Nicholson and raised his fist. He was trembling.

Nicholson stared back stonily. 'Shut up or you might get the same.'

Jill had knelt down by Emil. He spat a tooth out. It looked like a little torn radish lying in a spot of blood on the gravel. She wiped his mouth with a handkerchief and he said something.

She looked up at them and said, 'It's all right. It's one they'd broken already.'

Pickup nerved himself. He said, 'If he doesn't come, I don't.'

Nicholson stared at him, unwinding the webbing strap from his hand. He said, 'Let's be on our way.' He unstrapped the spare can of petrol from the running board and tipped it into the tank.

# CHAPTER 12

The lake stretched away until it merged with the grey dawn sky. The town climbed up from the shore, huddled houses nearest the water giving way to the long sloping planes of factory roofs. Surmounting everything was the slim tracery, indistinct in the morning haze, of the mast at which, Pickup knew – looking for it and finding it with a tiny thrill of satisfaction in some corner of his mind that was still open for normal Pickup business – the Zeppelins had moored.

It was two hours until the ferry sailed. He closed his eyes and thought, if only the Zepps *were* still flying. He saw the silvery shape gently tugging at and nosing back to the mast. They would go abroad: himself and Jill, in that flying skirt and hat she'd worn that first day she called for them in Munich, her eyes dancing; Nick, laughing and care-free again, just a neat, clean bandage on his head; Nicholson; oh, and Emil, of course, if a nicer, more gracious, more Christ-like Emil ... he saw the captain greeting them, dapper beard above a prim wing collar. They were lifting majestically, the crews on the handling ropes dwindling to tiny upward staring faces ... now the propellers spun sigmas of light, driving them smoothly upwards and onwards ... in the dining-room they sat by a wide, inclined window looking down on the receding fields ... a smiling steward poured coffee from a silver pot into straw-coloured cups edged with gold, crested in blue...

A fairy story came back to him. It must have been stirred up with all the other child-hood memories during the night: about some children trapped deep in Witchland but they'd escaped on the back of a great bird. When it reached safety it sprawled on the ground exhausted by the long flight. There'd been a picture of the children standing round and making a fuss of its lugubrious head. It had been the tiny Pickup's favourite hero. Well, there was no bird for them now. The Zeppelin age had ended in the frightful fire he'd seen on the newsreels as a sixth-former. There was only the steamer across the lake to Switzerland and the vons and zus' A.D.A.C. handbook was out of date like everything else about them. The first sailing wasn't until 8 a.m. in winter, which was an hour and a half, perhaps two hours, after the roll-call would have been called at Dachau. Already the telephone wires could be humming ... he felt sick and cold and small.

They were parked in the bleak square opposite the harbour station. It was foolhardy in a way but Nicholson had reasoned that wherever they abandoned the Horch it would soon enough be spotted if the police were looking for it, and there wasn't much else they could do with Nick except keep him warm in the car. He slept still. What could be seen of his face was pretty grey. The bandage was stained a rusty brown. Nicholson had unfolded a map and was studying it. The kid Emil had been persuaded to wait until they could buy their tickets and turn over to him what money remained.

Pickup looked out of the window again and started. 'I say, Ian!' He pointed across the square. A fawn saloon had parked close to the station entrance. 'That couldn't be ... could it?'

Nicholson looked over the top of the map. He said, 'I think it probably is. Duncoloured Peugeot. There could hardly be two alike around here.'

They watched for a while. A man and later

a woman got out. They seemed to be rummaging around in the back. A suitcase was lifted out which the woman took back into the front with her. The man followed with an armful of what looked like clothes again. Pickup had an intuition.

'Do you think they could be – you know, Jews?'

'Trying to get away, too?'

'Yes.'

He shrugged. 'It's possible.'

Another ten minutes dragged by.

Jill said, as if she'd just remembered, 'Do you know what Kurt wanted? He only wanted me to sleep with him after his silly midnight business. Said it was to complete his becoming a full-blown officer and man, in that order.' She scratched a match to light a cigarette. 'I suppose I might if it hadn't been for you lot.'

Pickup was filled with a deep and final melancholy.

Nicholson folded the map. He said, 'I've decided something, so I don't want anyone to argue. I've got you this far. Now listen. I'm not going on the ferry with you. Emil or whatever his name is will go instead. He can have my passport–'

They chorused their objections. 'He

doesn't want to go,' said Jill. 'What are you going to do?' demanded Pickup.

'Just a–'

'And anyway your photograph's in your passport.'

'I said *listen*, would you please? About the photograph: you've got one messed-up victim of a car crash. Have another. Stick some bandages on him. The build and colouring are about right. If they don't believe you there's a fifty-fifty chance they'll check up on Nick first, which would convince them pretty damn quick.' He looked at Emil as if assessing, at a low value, the bristling skull, the dumb brown eyes and squat nose, the puffy lip that he had helped produce. 'He's not exactly the ideal chap I'd choose to lend my identity to, but as you observed, Mickup, he's all we've got to show for the whole damfool stunt.' He paused as if he knew Pickup would have no reply to that.

'As for not wanting to go, I think we have some say in this matter. We risked our necks to organise the escape. He took advantage of it. Now it's up to him to go through with it. Tell him that, Jill. He's some sort of witness, isn't he? Well, he should have plenty to bear witness about. As to me: I had a chat with Helmuth. From the other end of the

287

lake, or a bit beyond, there are some nice little climbs into the mountains from which it's not too difficult to nip across the frontier. I know the country from the other side, actually. My father used to take me hill walking round Schaffhausen. I shall rather enjoy it.'

They looked at him uncertainly. He held up his hand to emphasise that he wasn't finished.

'But the most important point is something else altogether. Throughout this enterprise, bloody chaotic as it's been – excuse me, Jill – we've always observed the longstop rule. We had you, Mike, keeping watch outside the camp when Nick and Phil went in. We had me ready to dive into the consulate if I didn't hear from you. We sent Phil off yesterday, and the reason that we've got as far as we have may well be that at least the BBL end has been looked after. I can see you on to the boat and see it on its way, and if anything goes wrong I might still be able to organise something.'

Pickup couldn't think what to say. He didn't even know what to think.

Nicholson said briskly, 'I shall want that wind-jacket thing of Nick's. My shoes aren't bad. Has anyone got any good long socks?

Mickup, you might let me have your sweater. By the way, you'll be captain now. All right?'

Chill morning air blew in through the smashed window. The ambulance men had manoeuvred their blanket-draped stretcher down the stairs. The detective looked round the little room. He noted the bedding on the floor, the empty flagon, the bowl, the newspaper tamped into the window frame. Crossing to the window, for it was the routine not to switch on the electric light, even, until all the gas had dispersed, he reread the letter he had found on the mantelpiece. He skipped over the first paragraph, and also one which referred to some property in Germany and gave the name and address of a legal person in the country. He was puzzled by the last part.

Now I must take my leave. I shall not trouble you with further excuses. I ask you only to believe that the attacks of melancholy which have afflicted me since my release from protective captivity have become ever deeper, while the intervals between them have become shorter. I had hoped that the writing down of my story might help to free me from my despair, but this does not seem to be the case. K. sometimes argued that the only real release from Dachau lay in death. I did not know how truly he spoke, nor how baleful that place that it could even exercise its power over those who have physically departed. 1000 Km away, I hear the siren for roll-call and go to answer my name. Kind benefactor, farewell.

The detective put the letter in his pocket and went to see if the landlady in the basement had made a cup of tea.

The harbour station was cavernous, gloomy, cold. A handful of passengers were plodding away from the single drab-red railcar which had just drawn punily into a bay that would have taken the Orient Express.

Nick leaned heavily on Pickup, whether from need or for the sake of the performance Pickup did not know. Jill held Emil's arm to guide him. They'd swathed the top of his head in Nick's old rust-stained bandage, covering his eyes altogether. With his swollen lip he looked convincing enough; whether what was left showing of him sufficiently matched the stern features that gazed out from Nicholson's passport was another matter... Jill had given Nick a new bandage, much smaller. It revealed areas of brow stained yellow with iodine or something. And she'd improvised a sling for the injured hand.

Nick said, 'What about changing money? Do we change our money?' People off the train were going through a door marked WECHSEL.

Nicholson had taken most of what was left after buying their tickets but they were keeping a few marks for eventualities.

Jill said, 'We have to. They're fanatical about taking out Reichsmarks.'

Pickup took his place in the line waiting inside the change office. When his turn came the clerk looked at him blankly.

'What must we do? We are leaving, you see.' He felt naked, hopeless, had a wild impulse to own up, to blurt everything out. And this was only a bank clerk! How would he ever face the more fearful scrutinies to come? The clerk held out a hand for his passport, returned it. Counted the notes, rejected the small change, scribbled some figures into a printed form and passed it for Pickup to sign. Then he pushed across a single Swiss banknote and a heavy silver coin engraved on its rim. Pickup nodded and moved on, fumbling his passport back in his pocket, clutching the coin in his hand, feeling for the first time a rise of hope, as if the coin were a talisman, a tiny piece of the other world across the lake.

Outside again, the others had not moved. Nick was huddled on the bench. Emil sat upright, motionless. Nicholson looked up at the clock on the wall. He said, 'Thirty minutes. I think you should go through now.'

'You don't think it would be better to wait until the last minute – when they might be busier?' Even as he said it, he knew he didn't want to wait: he wanted to get it over, now, at once–

It was all right. Nicholson was shaking his head. 'They don't work that way.' He stuck out his hand. 'Well cheero, Mickup. Take care of them.'

Pickup's eyes smarted, of course. 'You look after yourself, more to the point.'

'Oh, I shall be all right. If the weather clears it should be a pleasant stroll.' He slapped Nick lightly on the back. 'On your way, Nick. See you back in Cambridge.'

Nick nodded his head slowly. His voice had become more like his accustomed voice. He said, 'We'll celebrate, won't we? I'm sorry about getting sloshed…'

'You had some cause to. And Jill—'

She took his hand in both hers but didn't kiss him, She said, 'You've been marvellous – of course.'

Nicholson said, 'I'll watch you sail. I'll be on the quay – along there beyond the Customs area.' He turned his back and walked away.

Pickup took Nick's arm. Jill said, 'Here goes then.' They followed a traveller in a leather motor cycling helmet, the earflaps hanging loosely, through the door marked PASSKON-TROL and Pickup's heart plummeted, for within the narrow chamber that lay beyond waited, motionless, all those they had watched go through earlier. The moment for which he had nerved himself was no nearer.

Minutes dragged by. He heard Nick muttering under his breath: Was it a prayer? Jill tilted her chin as if strength of personality would gain the day. Emil waited with the impassivity he had displayed ever since Nicholson hit him.

In the queue ahead he recognised the people from the Peugeot. The man was bald except for a fringe of dark, rather crinkly hair; not terribly old, say about forty; horn-rimmed specs and sallow complexion. His overcoat had a fur collar. The woman wasn't pretty as a girl could be pretty but attractive enough in the way that film stars were supposed to be attractive. Even in this gloomy cavern she wore sun-glasses. They had a great heap of luggage with them, all sorts of cases and baskets. The man did look Jewish, he supposed, but not the woman, really ... at this moment the man saw his gaze and returned it. For a second they stared across the hall at each other. Pickup thought, it's as if each guessed the other's secret. He looked away.

At last there was activity at the head of the line. A green-uniformed official had appeared behind a low table. Pickup saw him studying a sheet of paper which he laid down carefully again on the table before accepting the first proffered pass. He heard the low, grunted, catechism of frontiers everywhere.

A second official appeared, buttoning his tunic as he came. The line of waiting people shuffled forward a yard. Now a third figure, and Pickup thought, with a kind of dull relief that the suspense was over, it was all up: the newcomer's uniform was the black of the S.S. frontier guard. He stood behind the two officials, not helping with their routine work but staring arrogantly at the line of would-be travellers. As Pickup watched he swivelled his stare in their direction – Pickup looked down and away. He found himself regarding Emil's feet, shod still in those great boots. How silly that no one had noticed before.

He became aware of Jill nudging him. He looked up, and past her. One of the officials had come down the line and was addressing them. He stammered, 'What is it?' then realised that Jill was already replying in husky German. The official listened with a frown. He had a face like a wedge, wide at the eyes, narrowing curiously to a little pointed chin. He said something more and pointed up the room.

Jill said, 'We're to go up.' Seeing his expression, or perhaps Nick's, she added, 'It may be all right. He's worried about invalids having to stand and wait.'

They pushed to the head of the line. Pickup kept his eyes averted as they passed the Jewish couple. The official who'd summoned them reached for their passports. As he leafed through them he asked Jill another question, evidently about the accident, for she gestured vividly with her hands, making one tilt into the other. Pickup stared at the four little blue booklets, trying to determine which was Nicholson's. He saw the official look up, look at him, look down again.

Another voice: unexpectedly high, even squeaky. It came from the S.S. man. He was dark, with heavy jowls and a neck that creased over his tight collar. Pickup thought, this is the bully; at last I face him.

He looked into little suspicious eyes that reminded him of one of the stupidest louts in the fifth form at school. They switched away to look at one of the others, came back to him. The squeaky voice phrased a question. On the final vowel his lower lip stuck out like the lip of a jug. The fifth-form yob's had done that, too. His breath smelt of fish and stale beer and tobacco.

Jill whispered, 'He wants to know if we have a police clearance from the accident.'

'Tell him we were only passengers in someone else's car.'

The face listened without change of expression. The hand – coarse and hairy – shuffled the passports. Pickup knew with dreadful certainty that he was looking for Nicholson's. A thumb that must have been injured once, the nail grew as a thick yellow spike, forced the pages apart. There was Nicholson's picture, the Foreign Office stamp embossed across one corner–

The stupid eyes flicked up not at Emil but at HIM. Pickup did the only thing he could do: pretend indifference. He yawned and looked back down the hall. He saw the Jewish couple watching them intently: a fellow-feeling again, perhaps–

The S.S. man must have followed his gaze. He gave a sort of growl, thrust the passport back to the wedge-faced official and advanced down the line. Pickup saw the Jew man flinch. The woman put her hand to her mouth. He heard the S.S. man begin to shout.

He felt Jill nudging him. A voice was murmuring 'Bitteschön.'

'What?'

Their passports were being handed back. Unbelievingly he reached for them. The official tried some English: 'I am sorry you have had such – a bad luck in our country. I hope you come back another time.'

The white schloss and the two onion towers of its attendant church faded gradually into the haze. The Dornier works along the shore had already disappeared. Only the Zeppelin mast was still visible. From somewhere in the mist a lighthouse winked a red signal.

Small white waves covered the lake surface.

The Jewish couple had not caught the boat. That was all they knew. Nicholson had stood, an upright figure along the quay, until a quarter of a mile separated them from the land. The others were below. Pick-up peered ahead to see if the opposite shore were visible yet. It wasn't. He looked back at Germany. He resolved, I'll be back another time all right. In a Vickers-Supermarine Spitfire with Rolls-Royce Merlin engine of one thousand horse-power, eight forward-firing Browning machine-guns. *Ratatatata-tatat. Ratatatatatat.* He had looked into the face of the bully, and like the face of every bully it was stupid. It was thick from the neck upwards! He was famished, and thought, on the train to Zurich we will have coffee and rolls.

## AUTHOR'S NOTE

The title of this story is, I hope, the only bit of hindsight. The night of November 9th-10th, 1938, subsequently became known as *Kristalenacht,* the destruction of five million Reichsmarks' worth of Jewish windows being perhaps the most widely noticeable consequence. In addition two hundred synagogues and a thousand shops and houses were set on fire, and twenty thousand Jews arrested. The affair has been well chronicled by Lionel Kochan in *Pogrom* (Andre Deutsch). The evidence is that it was systematically inspired by Goebbels and Himmler taking advantage of vom Rath's death, and had very little spontaneity.

P.P.

This Large Print Book, for people
who cannot read normal print,
is published under the auspices of

## THE ULVERSCROFT FOUNDATION